THE MEAGRE TARMAC

TORONTO
PUBLIC
LIBRARY
Sale of this book
supports literacy programs

CLARK BLAISE

THE MEAGRE TARMAC

STORIES

BIBLIOASIS

Copyright © Clark Blaise, 2011

All rights reserved. No part of this publication may be reproduced
or transmitted in any form or by any means, electronic or mechanical,
including photocopying, recording, or any information storage and
retrieval system, without permission in writing from the publisher.

FIRST EDITION

Library and Archives Canada Cataloguing in Publication

Blaise, Clark, 1940–
The meagre tarmac / Clark Blaise.

Short stories.
ISBN 978-1-926845-15-9

I. Title.

PS8553.L34M42 2011   C813'.54   C2011-900983-8

Canada Council
for the Arts

Conseil des Arts
du Canada

Canadian
Heritage

Patrimoine
canadien

ONTARIO ARTS COUNCIL
CONSEIL DES ARTS DE L'ONTARIO

Mixed Sources
Cert no. SW-COC-001271
© 1996 FSC

FSC

We gratefully acknowledge the support of the Canada Council for the
Arts, Canadian Heritage, and the Ontario Arts Council for our publishing
program.

PRINTED AND BOUND IN CANADA

To my Granddaughter, Priya Blaise
For fifty years of guidance, all my Indian friends,
and of course my wife, Bharati.

CONTENTS

These stories are intended to be read in order.

The Sociology of Love   9

In Her Prime   24

The Dimple Kapadia of Camino Real   38

Dear Abhi   49

Brewing Tea in the Dark   66

The Quality of Life   78

A Connie da Cunha Book   97

Waiting for Romesh   113

Potsy and Pansy   125

Isfahan   147

Man and Boy   163

THE SOCIOLOGY OF LOVE

A MONSTROUSLY TALL GIRL from Stanford with bright yellow hair comes to the door and asks if I am willing to answer questions for her sociology class. She knows my name, "Dr. Vivek Waldekar?" and even folds her hands in a creditable *namaste*. She has researched me, she knows my job-title and that I am an American citizen. She's wearing shorts and a midriff-baring T-shirt with a boastful logo. It reads, "*All This and Brains, Too*." She reminds me of an American movie star whose name I don't recall, or the California Girl from an old song, as I had imagined her. I invite her in. I've never felt so much the South Asian man: fine-boned, almost dainty, and timid. My wife, Krithika, stares silently for several long moments, then puts tea water on.

Her name is Anya. She was born in Russia, she says. She has Russian features, as I understand them, a slight tilt to her cheeks but with light blue eyes and corn-yellow hair. When I walk behind her, I notice the top of an elaborate tattoo reaching up from underneath. She is a walking billboard of availability. She says she wants my advice, or my answers, as a successful South Asian immigrant on problems of adjustment and assimilation. She says that questions of accommodation to the u.s., especially to California, speak to her. And specifically South Asians, her honors project, since we lack the demographic residential densities of other Asians, or of Hispanics. We are sociological anomalies.

It is important to establish control early. It is true, I say, we do not swarm like bees in a hive. "Why do you criticize us for living like

9

Americans?" I ask, and she apologizes for the tone of her question. I press on. "What is it we lack? Why do you people think there is something wrong with the way we live?"

She says, "I never suggested anything was wrong – " She drops her eyes and reads from her notes.

" – That there's something defective in our lives?"

"Please, I'm so sorry."

I have no handkerchief to offer.

Perhaps we have memories of overcrowded India, when every-one knew your business. I know where her question is headed: middle-class Indian immigrants do not build little Chinatowns or barrios because we are too arrogant, too materialist, and our caste and regional and religious and linguistic rivalries pull us in too many directions. She hangs her head even before asking the next question.

No, I say, there are no other South Asian families on my street. My next door neighbours are European, by which I mean non-specifically white. I correct myself. "European" is an old word from my father's India, where even Americans could be European. Across the street are Chinese, behind us a Korean.

That's why I'm involved in sociology, she says, it's so exciting. Sociology alone can answer the big questions, like where are we headed and what is to become of us? I offer a counter-argument; perhaps computer science, or molecular biology, or astronomy, I say, might answer even larger questions. "In the here and now," she insists, "there is only sociology." She is too large to argue with. She apologizes for having taken my name from the internal directory of the software company I work for. She'd been an intern last summer in our San Francisco office.

I say I am flattered to be asked big questions, since most days I am steeped in micro-minutiae. Literally: nanotechnology. I can feel Krithika's eyes burning through me.

The following are my answers to her early questions: We have been in San Jose nearly eight years. I am an American citizen, which is the reason I feel safe answering questions that could be interpreted by more recent immigrants as intrusive. We have been married twenty years, with two children. Our daughter Pramila was born in Stanford University Hospital. Our son Jay was born in JJ Hospital, Bombay, seventeen years ago. When he was born I was already in California, finishing my degree and then finding a job and a house. My parents have passed away; I have an older brother, and several cousins in India, as well as Canada and the U.S. My graduate work took four years, during which time I did not see Krithika or my son. Jay and Krithika are still Indian citizens, although my wife holds the Green Card and works as a special assistant in Stanford Medical School Library. She will keep her Indian citizenship in the event of inheritance issues in India.

Do I feel my life is satisfactory, are the goals I set long ago being met? Anya is very persistent, and I have never been questioned by such a blue-eyed person. It is a form of hypnosis, I fear. I am satisfied with my life, most definitely. I can say with pride and perhaps a touch of vanity that we have preserved the best of India in our family. I have seen what this country can do, and I have fought it with every fibre of my being. I have not always been successful. The years are brief, and the forces of dissolution are strong.

Jay in particular is thriving. He has won two Junior Tennis Championships and maintains decent grades in a very demanding high school filled with the sons and daughters of computer engineers and Stanford professors. As a boy in Dadar, part of Bombay – sorry, Mumbai – I was much like him, except that my father could not offer access to top-flight tennis coaching. I lost a match to Sanjay Prabhakar, who went on to the Davis Cup. "How will I be worthy?" I had asked my father before going in. "You will never be worthy of

Sanjay Prabhakar," he said. "It is your fate. You are good, but he is better and he will always be better. It is not a question of moral worth." I sold my racquet that day and have never played another set of tennis, even though even now I know I could rise to the top of my club ranks. I might even be able to beat my son, but I worry what that might do to him. I was forced to concentrate on academic accomplishment. In addition, public courts and available equipment in India twenty-five years ago left much to be desired.

Do I have many American friends? Of course. My closest friend is Al Wong, a Stanford classmate, now working in Cupertino. We socialize with Al and Mitzie at least twice a month. She means white Americans. Like yourself? I ask, and she answers "not quite." She means two-three-generation white Americans. Such people exist on our street, of course, and in our office, and I am on friendly terms with all of them. I tell her I have never felt myself the victim of any racial incident, and she says, I didn't mean that. I mean instances of friendship, enduring bonds, non-professional alliances ... you know, friendship. You mean hobbies? I ask. The Americans seem to have many hobbies I cannot fully appreciate. They follow the sports teams, they go fishing and sailing and skiing.

In perfect frankness, I do not always enjoy the company of white Americans. They mean well, but we do not communicate on the same level. I do not see their movies or listen to their music, and I have never voted. Jay skis, and surfs. Jay is very athletic, as I have mentioned; we go to Stanford tennis matches. I cannot say that I have been in many American houses, nor they in mine, although Jay's friends seem almost exclusively white. Jay is totally of this world. When I mention Stanford or Harvard, he says *Santa Cruz, pops.* He's not interested in a tennis scholarship. He says he won the state championship because the dude from Torrance kept double-faulting. Pramila's friends are very quiet and studious, mostly

Chinese and Indian. She is twelve and concentrates only on her studies and ice-skating. I am not always comfortable in her presence. I do not always understand her, or feel that she respects us.

We will not encourage Pramila to date. In fact, we will not permit it until she is finished with college. Then we will select a suitable boy. It will be a drawn-out process, I fear, but we are progressive people in regard to caste and regional origins. A boy from a good family with a solid education is all we ask. If Pramila were not a genius, I would think her retarded. When she's not on the ice, she lurches and stumbles. Jay does not have a particular girlfriend. He says don't even think of arranging a marriage for me. Five thousand years of caste-submission will end here, on the shores of the Pacific Ocean.

"So, you and your son go to Stanford to watch Mike Mahulkar?"

"Mike?" I must have blinked. "It is Mukesh," I say. "My son models his tennis game on Mukesh Mahulkar. Some day Mukesh will be a very great tennis player." Neither my son nor I would ever be able to score a point off Mukesh Mahulkar.

My father has been dead nearly twenty years. I think he died from the strain of arranging my marriage. Krithika's parents never reconciled to my father's modest income. In my strongest memory of him, he was coming from his bath. It was the morning of my marriage. His hair was dark and wet. We will never be worthy, he said. A year later, I was sharing a house with Al Wong and two other Indian guys. Jay was born that same year, but I was not able to go back for the birth, or for my father's funeral services. Fortunately, I have an older brother. My father was Head Clerk in Maharashtra State Public Works Department. In his position, he received and passed on, or rejected, plans for large-scale building and reclamation projects. Anywhere in Asia, certainly anywhere in India in the past twenty years, such a position would generate mountains of black money.

Men just like my father pose behind the façade of humble civil servant, living within modest salaries, dressed in kurta and pajama of rough khadi, with Bata sandals on their dusty feet. They would spend half an hour for lunch, sipping tea under a scruffy peepal. But in the cool hours of morning or evening, there would be meetings with shady figures and the exchange of pillow-thick bundles of stapled hundred-rupee notes. They would be pondering immense investments in apartment blocks and outlying farmhouses and purchasing baskets of gold to adorn their wives and daughters.

But Baba was one of the little folk of the great city, an honest man mired in universal graft. He went to office in white kurta. At lunch, he sat on a wall and ate street-food from pushcart vendors and read his Marathi paper. He came home to a bath and prayer, dinner and bed. Projects he rejected got built anyway, with his superiors' approval. He was seen as an obstruction to progress, a dried-up cow wandering a city fly-over. So we never got the car-and-driver, the club memberships and air-conditioning. He retired on even less than his gazetted salary, before the Arab money and Bombay boom.

I suddenly remember Qasim, the Muslim man whose lunch cart provided tea and cigarettes and fried foods to the MSPWD office-wallahs. My father and Qasim enjoyed a thirty-year friendship without ever learning the names of one another's children, or visiting each other's houses, or even neighborhoods. Dadar and Mahim are different worlds. We never learned Qasim's last name. But whenever I dropped in on my father on lunch or tea breaks, I would hear him and Qasim engaged in furious discussions over politics, Pakistan, and fatherhood. Qasim had four wives and a dozen children, many of them the same age, all of them dressed in white, carrying trays of water and tea. Qasim and Baba were friends. To me, they are the very model of friendship. You might find it alien. You might not call it friendship at all. If, as rarely happened, Qasim did not appear on a given day, my father would ask a Muslim in the office to inquire after his health. Once or twice in a year, when my father took leave to attend a wedding, a strange boy would appear at our door, asking after Waldekar-sahib. I'm certain my father expressed more of a heartfelt nature to Qasim than he ever did to his wife, or to me. In that, I am my father's son.

"My father, too," says the blue-eyed girl in the T-shirt. *All This and Brains, Too.* Suddenly, I understand its meaning, and I must have uttered a muted "ahhh!" and blushed. Breasts, not height and blondness. I feel a deep shame for her. Krithika reads the same words, but shows no comprehension. I have a bumper sticker: *My Son Is Palos High School Student of the Month.* When I put it on, my wife said I was inviting the evil eye. For that reason, we have not permitted newspaper access to Pramila. We are simple people. Our children consume everything. To pay for tennis and ice-skating lessons takes up all our cash. I could have bought a Stradivarius violin with what I've spent. When Pramila was ten years old, after a summer spent in Stanford's Intensive Mathematics Workshop with the cream of the nation's high school seniors, she wrote a paper on the Topology of Imaginary Binaries. It is published in a mathematical journal, which we do not display. I do not mention it, ever.

"My father says that if he'd stayed in Russia and never left his government job, he would be sitting on a mountain of bribes. Over here, he started a Russian deli on Geary Boulevard."

"You have made a very successful transition to this country," I say. *All this.* "I personally have great respect for the entrepreneurial model."

She takes the compliment with a shy smile. "Appearances can lie, Dr. Waldekar," she says.

Krithika brings out water and a plate of savories.

I am of the Stanford generation that built the Internet out of their garages. I knew those boys. They invited me to join, but I was a young husband and father, although my family was still in India waiting to come over, and I had a good, beginning-level job with PacBell. I would be ashamed to beg start-up money from banks or strangers. My friends said, *well, we raised five million today, we're on our way!* And I'd think *you're twenty-five years old and five million dollars in debt? You're on your way to jail!* I have not been in debt a single day of my life, including the house mortgage. It all goes back to my father in frayed khadi, and three-rupee lunches under the dusty peepals.

"I notice an interesting response to my question," she says. "When I asked if you've fulfilled your goals, you mentioned only that your son is very successful. What about you, Dr. Waldekar?"

Krithika breaks in, finally, "We also have a daughter."

"I was coming to that," I say.

"She is enrolled in a graduate level mathematics course," says Krithika.

"That's amazing!"

"She is the youngest person ever enrolled for credit in the history of Stanford. She is also a champion figure skater. My husband forgot to mention her, so I thought you might perhaps note that, if you have space."

"I believe I mentioned she is very studious," I say. Suddenly my wife forgets the evil eye.

Anya breaks off a bit of halwa.

I rise to turn off the central AC. The girl is underdressed for air conditioning, and I am disturbed by what I see happening with her breasts, under the boastful logo. They are standing out in points. Krithika returns to the kitchen.

"I am content, of course." What else is there on this earth, I want to ask, than safeguarding the success of one's children? What of her father, the Russian deli owner? Is he happy? What is happiness for an immigrant but the accumulation of visible successes? He cannot be happy, seeing what has happened to his daughter. Does the Russian have friends? Does he barge into American houses? Do Americans swarm around his? Who are his heroes? Barry Bonds, Terrell Owens, Tiger Woods, Jerry Rice? We share time on the same planet; that is all. We will see how much the Americans love their sports heroes if any of them tries to buy a house on their street. Mukesh Mahulkar is big and strong and handsome and he is good in his studies and I'm sure his parents are proud of him and don't fear the evil eye. He'll play professional tennis and make a fortune and he won't spend it all on cars and mansions. He will invest wisely and he will be welcomed on any street in this country.

"My father works too hard. He's already had two heart attacks. My mother says he smokes like a fish. Drinks like a chimney. He dumps sour cream on everything. Everything in his mouth is salty, fatty meat, and more meat, and cream, and cheese and vodka. Forgive the outburst."

"We are vegetarian. We do not drink strong spirits."

"So's Mike. Veggie, I mean. He's teaching me."

"You mean Mukesh, the tennis player?"

"His name is Mike. He's my boyfriend, Dr. Waldekar."

The ache I feel at the mention of a boyfriend is like the phantom pain from a lost limb. If I could even imagine a proper companion for this Russian girl, he would be as white and smooth as a Greek sculpture, built on the scale of Michelangelo's David. The thought that it is a Mumbai boy who runs his hands over her body, under those flimsy clothes, makes my fingers run cold.

"I might as well come out with it, Dr. Waldekar," she says. "We've broken up. His parents hate my guts."

Good for them, I think. Maybe you should dress like a proper young lady. I knew a Mahulkar boy in Dadar. I knew others in IIT, but no Mahulkars of my generation in the Bay Area. So many have come. Given my early advantage, the opportunities I turned down, I am a comparative failure.

"This is my honors project, but ... it's personal, too. I love India and Indians, I love the discipline of Indians. No group of immigrants has achieved so much, in so little time, with such ease and harmony. I love their pride and dignity. I even love it that they hate me. I can respect it." She is smiling, but I don't know if I should smile with her and nod in agreement, or raise an objection. She might be a good sociologist, but there is much she is missing in the realm of psychology. So she goes on, and I don't interrupt.

"But what I don't love is that Mike won't stand up to them, for me. You know what his father said? He said *American girls are good for practice, until we find you a proper bride.* When Mike told me that, we laughed about it. I'm friendly with his sister and I said to her, *your game's a little rusty. Think you need some practice?* and we laughed and laughed. Mike said he'd show me Mumbai, and I said I'd take him to Moscow. He's twenty-two years old, but the minute his father said to stop seeing me, he stopped. One day we're playing tennis, or at the beach or he's cooking Indian vegetarian and I'm learning, and then, nothing. Nothing." She lets herself go, drops her head into the basin of her hands, and sobs. It is a posture I, too, am familiar with. Krithika rushes in from the kitchen, stops, frowns, then goes back inside. I will be questioned later: what did I do, say, what didn't I do, didn't say? She will suspect some misbehaviour.

So, I think, Mahulkar has found a bride for his son. This is very good news. Who could it be? Why hadn't I heard that the famous Mukesh Mahulkar was getting married? It means there is hope for every Indian father with a son like mine.

"Please, take water," I say. I would be tempted to hold her, or pat her back, but my arms might not reach. It would be awkward, and perhaps misinterpreted. Now that she has pitched forward, I see deep into her bosom; she has a butterfly tattoo on one breast, well below the separation-line. A girl this big, and crying, in my living room, wearing such a T-shirt, has brought chaos from the street into our life.

"I'm so sorry," she says. "That was inexcusable. You must think I came under false pretenses. Mike's getting married in Mumbai in three weeks. It's very hard, to be told, without warning, without explanation, that you're just ... unworthy."

She has a beautiful smile. It's as though she had not been crying at all, or knew no sadness, or had a Russian childhood and a father with a mouthful of meat and vodka. I will ask around and discover the bride's name.

I stand. "I must ask you quietly to leave. I must pick up my daughter from practice. My son will be home soon." I do not want her defiling my house, spreading her contagion into our sterile environment. She has no interest in successful immigrants, or in me. "I have no special Bombay advice to offer." When I open the door, my fingers brush the white flesh of her back, just above the tattoo. I don't think she even feels it. She says only, "you have been very kind and hospitable. Please forgive me."

I could not go home for my father's funeral. I did not see my son until he was four years old and had already bonded with my wife's family. I think he still treats me like an intruder. So does my wife. It has pained me all these years that I permitted my studies and other activities to take precedence over family obligations. I have been trying to atone for my indiscretions all these years.

In three of the four years I shared a house with Al Wong and the Mehta boy who went back and a Parsi boy who married an American girl and stayed, I remained steadfast to my research. I got a job at

PacBell, where they immediately placed me in charge of a small research cell with people like myself, debt-free, security-minded team players. Suddenly, I had money. I bought a car and a small bungalow in Palo Alto, suitable for wife and child. No one in the group knew I was already married, and a father. We were all just in our twenties, starting out in the best place, in the best of times.

In my small group there was an American girl, a Berkeley graduate. Her name was Paula, called Polly. Pretty Polly, the boys liked to joke, which embarrassed her. On Fridays, our group would join with others for some sort of party. I would allow myself a beer or two, since carbonation lessened the taint of alcohol. Those sorts of restaurants made vegetarianism very difficult; I was admired for my discipline. Polly was naturally less restrained than I, especially after sharing a few pitchers of beer, a true California girl from someplace down south. Watching closely, I could gauge the moment when a quiet, studious girl, very reliable and hard-working, would ask for a cigarette, then go to the bathroom, come back to the table, and sit next to someone new. She sat next to me. One night she said, "You're a very handsome man, Dr. Waldekar." No one had ever told me that, and to look fondly at one's reflection in a mirror is to invite the evil eye. "Take me home," she said. "I don't know where you live," I answered. She punched me on the arm. "Ha, ha," she said, "funny, too."

It's that transformation, not the flattery, that got to me. All week in the office, she was a flattened presence. She totally ignored me, and I, her. I imagined she was one of the good girls, living with her parents.

The passion that arises from workplace familiarity is hotter than hell. It *is* hell, because one must hide certain feelings, erase recurrent images, must put clothes back on a girl you've been with through the night. Above all, it must be secret. On Friday nights, she must not sit next to me. "May I call you Vivek, Dr. Waldekar?"

she would ask. After the first time, I told myself it was the beer, but I knew it wasn't. The sexual acts that had resulted in the birth of my son back in India, a boy whose pictures I now had to hide, had seemed, in comparison to Polly, a continuation of tennis practice, slamming a ball against a wall and endlessly returning it. She took drugs, expensive drugs, and I was helpless to stop her, or complain.

"Go to her, if that will make you happy," says Krithika. "I know your secrets."

"What foolishness."

"You were staring at her. You shamed me. You behaved disgustingly."

"If you were interested in the facts you would know I threw her out."

"Remember," she mumbles, "I get half."

I reach out for her, but she pulls away. This is the woman, the situation, I left Polly for. Eventually, I left PacBell because of her, which has worked out well for me. Polly left California because of me. Al Wong is the only person I confessed it to; I think he's mentioned it to Mitzie because of the ways she sometimes scrutinizes me. *What do you think of her, Vivek?* she'll ask me, as though I have a special interest in attractive women, instead of Al. Maybe she's mentioned it to Krithika. The promiscuous exchange of intimacies, which passes for friendship in America, is a dangerous thing. It is the sad nature of the terms of a marriage contract that the strongest evidence of commitment is also the admission of flagrant unfaithfulness.

One night fourteen years ago, I went up to SFO to meet Krithika and Jay who were arriving in my life after a thirty-hour flight from Bombay. I got there early and pressed myself close to the gate, but Sikhs from the Central Valley, rough fellows with large families and huge signboards, pushed me aside and called me names. It was a time of deep tensions between Hindus and Sikhs. If I had stood my ground, they threatened to stamp me into the floor. The Indian passengers poured through, fanning out in every direction, pushing carts stacked high with crates and boxes. Waiting families ducked under the barriers to join them, and I waited and waited, but no wife, no child. The terminal is always crowded, but the number of Indians diminished, to be replaced by Mexicans and Koreans. Perhaps she was having visa problems, I thought, or the bags had been lost.

After two hours, just as I'd decided to go back to my empty house, I heard my name on the public announcement. *Please pick up the courtesy phone, Vivek Waldeker.* Your wife wants you to know that since you were not here to meet them, she and her child have gone to a safe address provided by a fellow passenger, and she will contact you in the morning.

Two days later, I got that call. Perhaps you forgot you have a wife and son, she said. Perhaps you no longer remember me. She has remained on friendlier terms with that generous family who took her home on her first night in America than she ever has with me.

At four a.m. when the streets are dark and only the dogs are awake, the rattling of food carts begins. Barefoot men and boys dressed in white khadi push their carts heavy with oil, propane, and dozens of spiced tufts of chickpea batter ready for frying, all prepared during the night by wives and daughters. Each cart is lit by a naphtha lamp; each man fans out to his corner of the city near big office buildings, under his own laburnam, ashoka or peepal tree. Qasim died one morning as he pushed his cart through the streets of Mahim. His son Waqus appeared the next day, with his father's picture and a page of Urdu pasted to the cart's plastic shield. Even Hindus knew what it meant. My father took his retirement a month later – his superiors were truly sorry to see him go, since he was the obstruction that enriched everyone around him. He arranged my marriage, I received my Stanford scholarship and went to America, leaving a pregnant wife behind. After three years of bad health, Baba died. And I didn't attend the funeral services because I was trying to please an American girl who thought starting a fire in my father's body was too gross a sacrilege to contemplate.

IN HER PRIME

TIFFY HU AND I are passing by the hedges behind the tennis courts, headed to skating practice, when a horrible truth strikes me: life is eternal. There's no escaping it, not even in death. I'm scuffling my shoes over the concrete slabs, over tufts of grass and weeds and the anthills and dried snail shells. Dogs do their business under the hedges. Flies drop their eggs.

Smudgy little birds perch on the fence and hop through the thorny branches.

"You coming, Prammy?"

"I'm thinking," I say. What goes on in her little brain? It must be like the birds, hopping and chirping. Actually, I do know. It's sex, sex, sex.

A year ago, towards dusk, I was walking by this same place. A gray veil, like a frayed blanket, had moved up from the gutter and across the sidewalk. Birds were dive-bombing. As I got closer, the blanket dissolved into moving parts. Hundreds of mice, or maybe moles, were making a dash up from the sewers and across the naked sidewalk to their burrows under the hedge. It reminded me of a nature film, like wildebeest on their migration, attacked by crocodiles, or hatchling turtles pecked by seagulls.

We die and decompose. We never return and we will never sleep with virgins in a perfumed garden, or go to heaven or hell no matter what our sins or virtues, or drop into the airless nirvana my mother prays for. But this afternoon, the combination of birds and ants and tufts of grass makes me see that something of us does return. Our chemical shell is reabsorbed. It's as simple as the Law of Conservation of Matter. The elements keep going on, and on, and on and they recombine randomly, making birds and mice, grass and trees, and sometimes, even, every few thousands years I guess, a dog or a human being. Life is a default position. Wherever the promise of sustain-ability exists, something will find a way to inhabit it.

"Prammy?"

How many lives before I'm a self-conscious person again? There's no end to it until the sun quits, but then our elements are blasted into space and we drift in the dark for a few million years, like dandelion fluff, and our cells start splitting and a few billion years later we slither onto alien rocks in a galaxy far, far away. Without a gram of religious feeling in me, I'm suddenly a believer in eternal life. This is seriously weird.

The ice surface is a polished pearl, and I start by laying down a long, lazy sum, the ∫ from the Calculus, running the length of the rink, edge to edge. It's my signature: Pramila Waldekar was here. Nothing is hard if it can be reduced to numbers and everything, sooner or later, is just numbers. So long as I do my spins and axels inside the sum, I'll be safe. Today he's going to be hard on me, maybe because Tiffy is with me. "My Gods, you are not Aeroflot taking off from SFO, you are artist. You must rise from nuthink. From ice. All rise coiled inside."

And I wonder if there is not a coefficient that includes speed, drag, and vertical lift. It's a matter of directing energy.

Poor Borya thinks it's an invocation to the ∫-hole on the top of a violin, a subtle dedication to his marvelous self. Back in Minsk, he played the cello. Sometimes he plays for me.

People are prime numbers, or they're not. The Beast is eighteen, which factors to 3x3x2, a perfect expression of his mental age. I'm thirteen: prime. Tiffy Hu is twelve, 3x2x2: what more to say? Borya is thirty-seven: prime. We are irreducible. Borya hasn't been prime since he was thirty-one and he won't be prime again till he's forty-one. What will I be like in my next prime, at seventeen? A fat cow, says Borya. A woman is never stronger than she is at twelve or thirteen. We are designed for our maximum speed and strength, before the distraction of breasts and hips. He only takes on girls between eight and ten; after that their contours change, their centers of gravity, their strength. That's Borya's philosophy, and I endorse it.

He also says a thirteen-year-old woman will never be more desirable. It's a Russian thing, maybe. I've read *Lolita*. On a normal practice day, after skating, we drive to his place in Palo Alto and do it in his basement apartment, in the house of Madame Skojewska. Madame is the widow of Marius Skojewski, a Slavic Studies professor at Stanford. Borya says Polish ladies are "very tender, very sophisticated. Russian people very narrow, very brutal." In order to explain my comings-and-goings in Palo Alto, I asked Daddy to pay for Russian lessons, which he was happy to do.

Borya was surprised I wasn't a virgin. No girl with a brother like The Beast can be a virgin. No one watching us at the rink, listening to Borya's berating, his picking apart of my motivation, my technique, my discipline, would think us anything but bashful student and demanding teacher. With Tiffy Hu watching and waiting her turn, it's only skate, skate, skate: leap and twist and turn and spin, work up a sweat and then take her home with me for dinner.

The Beast is in. "Tiffy Hu!" he shouts, charming as always. "Hu's on first?" Tiffy doesn't get it. "Or should I be asking, who's first on Hu?"

"Ignore him," I tell her. "How's your Russian?" I ask. It's a test. If he suspected anything about Borya and me, he'd ask, *how's yours?*

He's got a Russian secret-girlfriend, a big golden Stanford soph-omore goddess, too good for his sorry UC-Santa Cruz freshman ass. I'm starting at Stanford next year, skipping the entire, doubtless illuminating, American high-school experience. I'll be the youngest they've ever admitted. I'll be thirteen years, ten months.

The Golden Goddess used to go with the big Stanford tennis player, Mike (that is, Mukesh) Mahulkar. The Beast used to be his lob-and-volley partner. The Beast was a decent high-school player – he even won the state finals. Golden Goddess would spread a towel on the grass and watch them slug it out. Those long, golden legs, those skimpy tops – I could see The Beast was a little distracted. Then suddenly Mike and GG were no longer a couple – Mike's par-ents said she was just another practice-partner – and Mike was engaged to a proper caste-and-class appropriate Bombay cutie. The Beast, just a senior in high school, started hanging out with GG. Our parents would have nailed his door shut if they'd known. At least it left me free to explore other options.

My father and The Beast think Mike Mahulkar is going to be the next Big Name in international tennis. No way, I say. I charted two of Mike's games. He's totally predictable. Backhand, forehand, lob, rush the net. So many balls to the net, so many deep volleys, side to side, in a sequence even Mike doesn't know is mathematically pre-dictable. You can lure him to the net and set him up for a passing shot. Of course The Beast can't, and so far no one in the amateur and college ranks can, but some Swede or Russian will humiliate him. I showed The Beast my pages of calculations. "Even you can beat him," I said. "Here's the probabalistic algorithm for beating Mike Mahulkar," and he said to me, "just go back to the ice."

The Beast thinks the only difference between him and Mike is Mike's superior coaching and Stanford's weight room and flexibility training. Since we didn't have our own gym and staff of coaches, he doesn't stand a chance against the famous Mike Mahulkar. So Mike is strong and determined, but just forget that his game is boring and he'll meet someone out there who matches him in strength and sees into his game and sends him spinning back to country club status and an eventual MBA.

We sit in silence around the dinner table. We always sit in silence. I cannot remember a time when anyone spoke. We're not like Americans, grabbing a bite here and there, stuffing ourselves with processed foods, injecting our flaccid bodies with empty calories in front of a television feeding us empty images. Therefore we are better than Americans with beef blood dripping from their fangs.

We never miss a meal. We are family. We are Indian. We are vegetarian. Every meal is a small production. Chop-chop, spice and dice, then fry, always fry. Even our bread and desserts are fried. Our walls glisten from airborne globules. My forehead glows. We sweat it. We practically bathe in vegetable oil. Our lifetime vegetable oil consumption, expressed as a function of water-use, is rising.

Of course I am the only true American in the family. The Beast was born in Bombay. He conveniently forgets this fact. I have my sliced red pepper, celery and carrots. Tiffy is scarfing down on the fried food.

She breaks the silence. "This is really good!" and my mother is pleased. This is the daughter she should have had. "All we get at home is greasy soup with noodles and pieces of vegetables swimming around in it."

I could say all we get is the same stuff, chopped and fried in the same spices, every day for all eternity. I stopped last year. His Lordship is drinking a beer. The Beast has a Coke; Tiff, Her Ladyship and I have iced tea.

"Chinese food is very good. I have many Chinese friends," says His Lordship. So far as I know, all he has is Al Wong, his friend since graduate school, and Al and Mitzi come over once a month and they go to Al and Mitzi's once a month, and they play bridge.

"Chinese food very healthy," says my mother.

"Especially deep-fried egg roll," says The Beast. *Don't say it*, I pray, but out it comes: "I mean egg loll and fly-lice." He never disappoints. Tiff doesn't get it.

"Chinese people are like Indian people," His Lordship explains. "Very loyal to family. Children very loyal to parents, parents very protective of their children."

Tiff looks to me for help. "I never thought of that," she says.

"I think we're very Greek, actually," I say.

Mother says, "Greek people eat meat wrapped in leaves."

"Greek myths," I say.

"What myths?" His Lordship weighs in. "All European myths are comic book versions of Indian myths."

"I was thinking of Atreus," I say, to deafening silence.

On the walk back, Tiff asks, "What's that Atreus thing you said?" Just the usual incest and slaughter, I answer. Gross, says Tiff. Then she says, "your dad and Al Wong actually rented a house in Palo Alto? Lots of hot action, I'll bet." Among Chinese, Al Wong is a little bit famous.

But she doesn't know my father. My father and hot action – in the linguistic interstices, all things are possible, I guess. And the third guy, a Parsi, went back to India. But then she says, "You won't get mad if I ask a personal question?" My life is nothing but very personal secrets. "Go ahead," I say.

"You and Borya, you're getting it on, aren't you?"

"Getting it on? What does that mean, exactly?"

"I don't care if you are or if you aren't. I was wondering about, you know, his thing. How big is it?"

"Big, meaning long, or wide, or what? It's a meaningless question, Tiff. Big as a function of his pinky finger? Big as a function of his arm?"

"Forget about it," she says. And I wonder if she already knows that she's next. And Tanya Ping is lined up, just after her. "Just, what's sex like?"

It's like a puppy of some rough, large breed that just keeps jumping up and licking your face. It's shaped like a candle, without a wick. Of course, Borya's Jewish, so the shape's a little off. "It makes you sleepy," I say and Tiff nods, "that's what I thought."

Maja Skojewska was Maja Pinska. "I grew up in a very liberal Jewish family," she told me, in our informal Russian "classes", and when I'm her age I'll probably be saying, "I grew up in a Hindu family." Madame's idea of Russian lessons is to talk of her life, in Russian, interjecting Polish and English and before too many weeks she says, "See? You just asked me that in Russian!"

Her father was a schoolteacher, a great admirer of India. That's why she and her sister, Uma, have Indian names. When the Germans came to the school to get him, the priest said, we already turned him over. And there he was all along, working in the same school, only sooty black from shoveling coal. The Germans couldn't imagine a Jew working like a Pole, dirtying his hands like a Pole. Her husband-to-be was also a schoolteacher, a Polish Catholic (not to be redundant) but after the war he went to university, then to Moscow State for more study and after two books, he was invited to Oxford, and that's when they made their escape. The idea that little Maja Pinska would be eighty years old and tending her garden in California is testimony, she says, to a kind of stubborn life force.

On her table are bananas so unblemished that I thought they were wax. "That's the first thing I noticed when we got to England," she says. Bananas! And the thrill of peeling a banana has never left her, after fifty years. And we sit a few minutes in silence, and she leans towards me and says (I'm sure it's in Russian, but it's as clear to me as English), "You know, Borya will drop you."

"I know," I say.

"I don't approve of what he does, but then I say, it's better you learn from him than from these boys I see on the streets."

"Yes," I say.

Sometimes I think of Madame's life, and mine, and that it's all a kind of trigonometry of history. Her life is a skyscraper, mine is just a thimbleful of ashes, but our angles are the same. My adjacent side is just a squiggle, and my opposite side barely rises above the horizon. But the angle is there. I feel that I can achieve monumental things if I can just live long enough.

Even with all his money, it took Al and Mitzi fifteen years to leave their cottage in Cupertino and splurge on a 23rd-floor apartment in downtown San Francisco. It's all glass, 360° panoramic views of the city, the Bay, the bridges, the Marin Headlands, Berkeley and Oakland. No interior walls, but for the bathroom and two bedrooms. They also have a country estate in Napa. Some evenings when the fog rolls in, we're suspended in a dream, disrupted only by bridge-table small talk. Other nights, the city sparkles. Al pours me a small glass of plum wine. Tonight, my father complains of his job. He's in nanotechnology, and his responsibilities are shrinking fast.

"Have you thought about something new?" Al asks. "I mean really new."

"Yes, I have," His Lordship responds. It's the first time I've ever heard such a thing. He always defends continuity. His father spent forty years in Maharashtra State Government service. What really new thing could he possibly do?

Every now and then, when Mitzi and Her Ladyship are out of the room, Al Wong will say, "What do you hear from our old friend?" He's got a needle, and he uses it. I can tell it's a jab to my father's self-esteem, but I don't know what it means. I think there's a lot of sado-masochism, not nostalgia, in their friendship. Sometimes it's good to be a quiet, studious, Indian daughter; I'm just furniture. Except for Borya and Madame, I'm accustomed to being ignored.

Most of the time, they just sit and complain, drink some wine and play their bridge. After half a glass, my mother will say, "What was the bid? I'm feeling so light-headed!" Al and my father were in grad school together and started out at PacBell together, and my father's still there. Al decided to go entrepreneur, and bought a computer franchise. He sold that at just the right time and bought and sold a few more things at their peak, and then he bought a hotel in Napa. He built it up with spas and a gourmet restaurant and hiking trails, and then he opened a winery: *AW Estates*. The hotel is where young Bay-Area Chinese professionals want to get married, or at least honeymoon or go on weekend getaways. He says there are so many young Bay-Area Asians at his hotel that it's like a second Google campus. *AW Estates* pinot is what young Chinese professionals drink. He's even got a line of plum wine for the older folks, a girl like me. Every thing he touches turns to gold.

I don't know how it started, but tonight there's an edge, an identifiable complaint, coming from my father. "I've been thinking," he starts, and he leans forward, perhaps aware that I'm sitting ten feet away. "I'm thinking my children disrespect me."

That's the news? Al says, "Mitzi and I never wanted children." Once they made that decision, she went to law school and now she's a major litigator.

"I blame this country," says my father.

"It's in the culture," says Al. He came from Hong Kong. "We can't live their lives."

"I believe my son is dating a person without my permission. I believe he is involved with a most inappropriate young lady."

That's when Al says, maybe to break up the seriousness, "By the way, guess who's back from the East? Now she's an accountant. I've hired her to do my books."

And then, just from His Lordship's grimace, it all makes sense. There *was* someone in those days of hot action in Palo Alto. Tiffy Hu smelled it out, and I've spent thirteen years in a fog. It's so exciting, so unexpected, I want to jump up and pump my fist.

"I think ..." my father says, then pauses, "I think that we must leave this country."

If furniture could speak, it would shout, "What?!"

"Hey, man, that's an extreme reaction," says Al.

"I'm not talking of that one. I have been a bad father. Things have been going on under my nose, outside my control. Asian children should never be allowed to stay in this country past their childhood. I may have already lost my son, but I can still protect my daughter. If I can save one from shame and humiliation I will at least have done half my job."

I clear my throat. "May I speak?"

His Lordship stares across the living room, as though an alarm clock he'd set and forgotten about had just gone off. Truly, I am invisible to him. "Pardon me, but that train has left the station."

"We're not talking of trains," he snaps.

"Okay. That horse has left the barn."

I never thought I would, under any circumstance, defend my brother. His Lordship, says, "Kindly keep your opinions to yourself. You are not part of this conversation. This is about your brother."

I'm up against something that is irrational. I can't argue against it. "No, it's not! It's not about him. That genie is out of the bottle. It's about me, isn't it?"

Al Wong passes his hand between my father's frozen gaze, and me. "Vivek," he says, "she has a point."

Some day I want to ask Al Wong, what was it that happened in that house in Palo Alto? What caused my father to cast a lifelong shadow on this family?

"Go to your mother," my father says.

I don't go directly to my mother. My fate in this family is, as they say, fungible. I approach the sofa where His Lordship is seated. "Let me say one more thing. If you try to make me go back to India and if you stop me from going to Stanford and you try to arrange a marriage with some dusty little file clerk, I'll kill myself."

Things have been frosty these past few days. The Beast is back in Santa Cruz. While I'm at work on my AP History, and my parents are watching a rented Bollywood musical, the phone rings and my father picks it up, frowns, then holds it out towards me. "It's your teacher," he says, and I expect a message from school, maybe an unearned day off, but it's Borya. He says, "Madame is asking for you."

I tell him I have no way of getting there. And why would she be asking for me?

"I am driving," he says, an amazing concession. He is not a hop-in-the-car Californian. He's a skater, not a driver. I didn't even know he has a license.

Normally, I would never ask to leave the house after dark, but when I say, "Madame Skojewska is asking to see me. Mr. Borisov will pick me up," my father barely lifts his eyes from the television.

"Where will you be?" he asks.

I write down Madame's address and phone number. They don't know that Borya lives in her basement.

I recognize the car as Madame's, usually parked and dusty in her garage. She revs the engine once a week. It's been over a year since she bought a gallon. "A gallon a year, if I need it or not," she joked.

Borya starts out in English, "We go to Stanford Hospital. Madame has ..." he strikes his chest, "heart." Stanford Hospital is where I was born, but this doesn't seem a commemorative moment. And then, it must have occurred to him that we are not at the ice rink and that no one is watching, and that my months of Russian instruction permits adult interaction; he grabs my hand, kisses it, and says, "you know how she loves her bananas. She walked down to Real Foods, bought two bunches, and on her walk back home she suddenly collapsed."

When we arrive at the hospital, he says "They said she was going, tonight."

She's in the ICU, under a plastic tent. It reminds me of the flaps on baby-strollers, the plastic visors, the baby warm, secure and sleeping while rain is pelting. Just like that, sweet mystery of life and death. One day we were chatting like old friends, *See, you just asked me that in Russian!* and I felt I belonged in a time and place I'll never see, *I've never had a student like you, you sit so quietly, you don't repeat words, you don't ask why we say it the way we do – you just start speaking it like a native, like someone reborn.*

A student like me is accustomed to praise from her teachers. But that's not the point; the point is, I impressed *her* and she's the only teacher I'm likely to remember. I remember years of teachers' meetings, standing alone at the edge of the classroom while a teacher pulls my parents aside. I see her gesturing, and my parents shaking their heads. *What did she say about me?* I ask when we're back home and my mother says, *Some nonsense*, and my father says *You have a good head, but you are prone to dreaming and you must work harder, or you will fail.* I know it's about the evil eye; I might accidentally hear some praise that will turn my head from proper feminine modesty.

"You know what she said about you, even today? Even this morning when she was headed out to buy her bananas? She said, 'Borya, living long enough to teach that girl Russian is the greatest privilege of my life.'"

We stand behind the glass and it seems that Madame's eyes are open, and shining. I raise my hand and flutter my fingers; it's all I can do. *Do svidaniya, Madame.*

I think I know what it was, back in that rented house in Palo Alto when my father and Al Wong and the Parsi guy were Stanford students and my mother and the baby Beast were still in India. Al knows, Mitzi knows, my mother knows. He wants to go back to India because someone from his past, a woman perhaps, has suddenly come back. Some long shadow of shame has shaped our lives. It's about him, not me, though I'm the one who will pay the price.

When Madame died, I started thinking of other teachers.

When I was very young – five, I'd guess, in pre-school – I discovered algebra. First, it was the word itself, it tasted good in the mouth, like something to eat or drink. Fortunately, I had a teacher, "Miss Zinny" we called her (I think her good name was Zainab, and we were the only two South Asians in that class), who didn't laugh when I asked her what algebra was. The next day she brought her college math book and we spent my naptime working out the problems. I remember the excitement, the *freedom* in a phrase like "*Let P stand for ...*" or a declaration like "*Let A=C+1.*" Solve for the value of C. The consolation of algebra; everything is equal to something else. It was something I couldn't explain, but it's what I felt a few years later when I learned about imaginary numbers. It's about seeing the nine-tenths of the iceberg, and not being afraid. What I remember is the equals sign. Everything in the world can be assigned a value, and has an equivalent. I went home and told my mother, "Let P stand for potato. Let R be rice."

"Then wash the rice, please," she said.

THE DIMPLE KAPADIA OF CAMINO REAL

MY HUSBAND IS IN INDIA. He says "back in India" and he'll call for me to follow as soon as he's found a job and a flat. It seems that I've spent my life waiting for his phone calls. Twenty years ago it was: *I have found a house for us. I have put in for your papers. You will be coming to California in three weeks. Tell Jay I've seen cowboys and Indians in California. Get a good new bag and pack it.* Now I wait for another call to put our Camino Real house on the market and take Pramila out of school and prepare her for a new life in India. There are many good convent schools, he tells me. I know there are many fine convent schools – I went to one at her age – but her needs are not like mine. She's supposed to start at Stanford next year, the youngest student (13 years, ten months) they've ever taken.

"She wants to go to Stanford for pride reasons only," my husband says. "She'll learn. Pride is not good in a girl."

He thinks he can make all of this happen while he's on his normal two-weeks' vacation and two additional weeks' deferred vacation-time. All the years we've spent here, and he still lives in the India we knew, when American dollars and a Green Card opened every door and "foreign-returned" meant you could command your destiny. Now Jay is going to university in Santa Cruz, and our daughter is starting at Stanford, and the Camino Real house is silent and even a little dusty because I don't see the need to keep it clean or even livable. Pramila barely eats, and I can get by on fruit and curd. Half the time, I don't know if she's home or not. No radio, no television. I miss the pounding of male urination, because with men around I know there's something predictable in the house.

Yesterday I went up to Macy's in San Francisco to replace a dead battery in my watch. Of course I didn't have to take a train to the city and there are places in Stanford and San Jose that are closer, but I don't associate San Jose with adventure and freedom, and these days I'm totally free, and restless. Macy's on Union Square was practically empty. A Mexican worker was polishing chrome and glass with just a squeegee bottle of blue liquid and a long rag. Salespeople were standing around in clumps of three and four and the islands of jewelry, the bottles of fragrance and the watches stood unattended. Only the Mexican kept moving and his polishing rag left a kind of glow behind him.

I had salad in the food court of the San Francisco Center. I looked inside a luggage store and remembered going to Crawford Market twenty years ago to buy my bag for America. It was my first case with hard sides and a lock. I remember the owner sending a little boy up a ladder to retrieve it, and then toweling off the dust and cobwebs. It cost a hundred rupees, back when rupees were five to a dollar. I still have it. It would cost four hundred dollars to replace it now.

I'm so rarely in San Francisco that I thought of calling up our oldest friends, Al and Mitzi Wong, but then I thought: why? They are actually my husband's oldest friends and maybe I should call them our only friends, because my husband is not a sociable man. Mitzi invited Pramila and me to move in with them for as long as my husband was away. They have a twenty-third floor loft in the middle of the city, shaped like the wedge of a pie. Imagine the part of the pie that falls over the edge of the pan as a solid wall of floor-to-ceiling

windows looking out over the Bay across to Berkeley and the hills –
and imagine the Bay flecked with sailboats and ferries crossing both
ways – and at the point of the wedge, where all the slices meet and
the juices come bubbling up, as a kind of circular lobby with chan-
deliers and leather chairs and your own media center called
"Cinema 23" stocked with dozens of DVDs just for the six owners on
the twenty-third floor. Al Wong also owns a hotel and winery in
Napa. They are very generous people, but how could we show up,
even if Pramila would come, with just my old Crawford Market
suitcase?

And, I must confess, it frightens me to look out their windows
and not see streets or trees or hedges or parked cars along a sidewalk – just the fog drifting by and on a clear day the Oakland hills.
Whenever we visit, I sit as far from the windows as possible with my
back turned to them, and my hands still perspire and I can barely
catch my breath. I think Pramila and Jay could sit on the window
ledge and swing their legs over it.

When my husband calls me, he says, the shops here are full. The
streets here are clogged. You can't imagine the prosperity of India.
There are so many new shopping malls that even the international
chains are put on waiting lists for floor space. There are signs in
every window begging for sales assistants. Escalators are so crowded you have to wait five minutes at the bottom to squeeze on to one.
Everyone is making money. Everyone is spending money.

But Bombay isn't cheap. It's more expensive than the Bay Area.
Even if we get two million for the Camino Real house, he's afraid
we'll have to cut back a little on accommodations in Bombay. No
garden. But we'll have a roomy apartment on a high floor, above
the street noise and pollution. Who needs air-conditioning when
you have genuine sea breezes? He's tried to make contact with some
of his old batch-mates, but they're all in Europe or America, except

for Sunil Marchandani, do I remember him? I don't recall the name, but apparently Sunil is high in the riggings of Birla Technology. They haven't got together yet, but my husband knows there will be an offer because he's Green Card with an American doctorate and twenty years' devotion to PacBell. In the current climate, I've heard, we'll be lucky to get a million-four.

My full name is Krithika, but he knows me as Kay. "Hello, Miss Kay," he usually says, and I answer, "Hello, Mr. Wally." He is Wally of "Sam and Wally's," the only grocery store within walking distance. He's usually outside tending the bushel baskets of fruit. Very good fruit, kept in the sunlight on the sidewalk, but not very good vegetables, kept inside on shaved ice. I don't drive, and when my husband is here he is a reluctant chauffeur, so I drop by the food store several times a week. Wally's cousin Harry runs the meat counter, so I have little contact with him. They're part of an extended family, or maybe they just came from the same West Bank village. His brothers are Christian, but some of his nephews are Muslim. Maybe they belong to the same tribe. Castes make sense to me, but tribes do not; maybe they're the same. Among themselves they speak Arabic, but to the customers they speak perfect English, like they've always been here.

The cash-register girls are Hispanic. Wally is Waleed. Sam is Sameer. Harry is Haris. They have full, fleshy, assertive faces and bushy, graying mustaches. They remind me of the handsomeness of Muslim actors on the screens of my youth, like Dilip Kumar or moderns we watch at night on DVDs, like Shah Rukh Khan.

I'm shopping for apples and Wally is out front, tossing out anything soft or bruised. I say tossing, but it's gentler than that, as though he's selecting fruits that are just slightly overripe but can still be used. Maybe he has a wife who said bring me the bruised fruit and I will bake a banana cake. Bring me figs, bring me peaches, I will make compotes and syrups to pour on ice cream. So I'm watching him, and he says, "Hello, Miss Kay. Let me make you a basket of fruits."

I'm not accustomed to personal attention, but today I smile and say, "thank you, Mr. Wally." His selection for me is ultra-careful. He seems to be talking to the fruit, not looking at me. "In Europe, shoppers aren't allowed to handle fruit. Here, they grab at it with their fingertips, like ice-tongs. Fruit has to be cradled. It's living flesh – you can't pinch it. Pressure leaves a bruise on ripe fruit. When I first came here I was shocked. I almost slapped their hands, like bad children." In ten seconds, I've learned more about him than I have in a dozen years. He laughs and hands me the small basket: apricots, nectarines, peaches, cherries and grapes. "Here, hand-selected. The best of the best."

"If only your vegetables were as good as your fruit," I say, laughing, and reach for the basket and my hand closes over his. He is slow to remove it. In confusion I ask, "Where were you in Europe?"

"Five years in Marseilles working for my uncle." He continues culling the peaches and nectarines. "Fruits need to ripen. Vegetables you want to keep from ripening. We got a new shipment today, you like Brussels sprouts? Artichoke? Cauliflower? Snowy white cauliflower. Come to the back with me." And we walk down the main aisle. He has his half-apron on; I'm carrying the basket of fruits with pictures of apples on the side, and he's still talking. "Miss Kay, you're bringing up all kinds of memories. When I was just a little boy, I used to save my money and spend it on Indian films. Yes, there was an Indian family in Nablus, and they owned a restaurant and a movie house. I loved those films. The Kapoors. Rajesh Khanna."

And then he does something very strange. He pivots, facing me, then throws his arms out straight like a scarecrow, and snaps his fin-

THE DIMPLE KAPADIA OF CAMINO REAL   43

gers. He's dancing. "Oh, and the heroines were so lovely!" I would never expect a word like lovely to come spilling out of a grocer. But he'd lived in France and I've never even visited. "Hema Malini ... Dimple Kapadia ..."

I have to giggle. Dimple Kapadia! I haven't thought of her in thirty years. My father, my sisters and I used to go to films every Saturday. When he was young, back in Aurangabad, he wanted to be an actor or singer and he learned to dance and he still sings ragas in the morning, but he went to Bombay and became a tooth-puller instead. For one bright year when Dimple Kapadia was sixteen and I was ten, she was the biggest star in my world. "Bobby" was the biggest movie of the year. That same year, she married the biggest star in Bombay, Rajesh Khanna, and my sisters and I would read the film magazines about his philandering and her unhappiness, raising her two daughters, one called Twinkle, while he cavorted around with other starlets. After the divorce, Dimple returned to films, still a star but more as a character actress. She once did a topless scene, which was a big scandal but I didn't see it.

"We knew India was a poor country like us, even poorer, but in the films everyone was happy and we knew that everything would turn out the way it should. I thought if I couldn't get to Europe or America, I would try to go to India."

What to say? We always thought that we would do anything to get out of India. We'd go to Zambia if we couldn't get to America. My father turned down fifteen marriage offers from four countries before selecting my husband.

"You know, Miss Kay, you have eyes like Dimple Kapadia." He says it directly to me, not to the bins of fruit, as close to me as an eye doctor. And then I did something I have never, ever thought of: I threw my arms around him and gave him a kiss, not an air-kiss on the cheek like I do with Al Wong, but a full, wet kiss on his thick lips, under his moustache. What is the purpose of explaining it? I simply did it. I had not planned it, nor did I even have the desire for it. It just happened. I bit the tip of his moustache.

"Come with me upstairs," he says, and I follow.

The word "seraglio" comes to mind, a word I've never heard, or used, but I think I know its meaning. Have I been banished to a seraglio, or did I, a free, forty-one-year-old woman, willingly allow myself to be swept up by passion? It is a room of rugs; Persian carpets double deep on the floor, durries on the walls and ceiling and draped across the bed and chairs. It is an urban tent on the second floor rear of a Palestinian-California grocery store. A fan throbs overhead. There is no window. When I go to rug stores I always feel like lying down on the pile of carpets; a tall stack of rugs is the perfect mattress. I grow drowsy in their presence; maybe there's something in the dyes that affects the eyes, or maybe it's something older and deeper, something ancestral perhaps, the memory of window-less tents and carpets. My Dimple Kapadia eyes are losing their luster, the eyelids are descending and I settle myself on the wondrous bed, plush with carpets.

He is over me, in me, around me, in seconds. My eyes are closed but I feel his hard hands and thick fingers unbuttoning my blouse, my skirt, and his hairy back, his mustache – the urgency – and I recognize that same thing in myself, I claw at everything I feel and I hear the popping of buttons, the ripping of cloth.

It's over so soon. Too soon, perhaps, but it doesn't matter. I've never been raised so high, at the top of a roller-coaster ride, but none of it matters. I've brought a hardened, calloused man to this, to his panting breath, the clutching at his chest, his smile.

"Ma!" Pramila calls, "for you." And there's a woman at my door, dark-haired but a little stout. Potato-shaped, I think. She's American, with no accent. We are rarely visited by Americans without accents unless they're selling something. "Hello, Mrs. Waldekar," she says, "my name is Paula, and I'm an old friend of Al Wong. May I come in?"

She seems harmless. I would call her fashionable, up to a point, wearing an expensive silk scarf pinned to one shoulder, but not particularly attractive. She says, "I was part of that original nanotech team at PacBell. That was then. Now, I'm Al's new accountant."

"Would you like tea?" I ask. "Juice?"

Her smile says no, not necessary. Pramila brings a glass of orange juice on a silver tray, just like a dutiful daughter well-trained in an Indian convent school. When we're seated she says, "PacBell was twenty years ago, how time flies."

"My husband was working on that project," I say. "Maybe you knew him?"

"Yes, indeed, Dr. Waldeker was my immediate superior. I went east after that, got married, took an MBA degree, jobs came, jobs went. Husbands came, husbands went, no children. Sort of typical for the times, I guess. I'm spending a few days reintroducing myself to old friends ... and new."

I tell her that I was in India at the outset of the project. The good old days of nanotech at PacBell, with Al-before-Mitzi. There was a third guy in the house my husband and Al rented, a Parsi fellow from Bombay, who drifted off.

"I know," she says. "Your husband talked about you, and – what was it – a son?"

Six months ago, she says, she decided she had never been happier than when she was in the Bay Area, and decided to come back. She called Al, and immediately he hired her as CFO of the many Wong Enterprises. I say I'm sure my husband would love to see her again, but he is in India.

"Al tells me Vivek's thinking of going back," she says.

So it's Vivek now, is it? I never use his good name myself.

"He's exploring all options," I say. Those are his words. This is a woman who knew my husband when I was still in India, waiting for the wave of his magic wand.

"I just wanted to say hello," she says. "Please let him know I'm back in the Bay Area."

Then she looks up at me and I see it all in front of me; she is twenty years younger, and could be quite attractive, even provocative. Less like a potato, and more like a carrot. I guess her to be maybe Jewish, and then I think of west-Asian types with their big dark eyes and heavy noses and puffy lips and of Mr. Wally and his brood of cousins and probably a wife who could look a lot like her.

"Is there anything else I should say?"

"He knew me back then as Polly Baden, a post-doc from Berkeley. Then – he'll get a kick out this – I was, fairly briefly, Polly Mehta, from Toronto. He was a wild Parsi guy, in case you're wondering. Now I go by the name of Paula McNally, from New Jersey." She looks down at her feet – she is wearing sandals, I notice, and her nails have been professionally trimmed and clear-polished – "who knows, maybe I'll pick up a third. The number of graduate degrees in one's life should at least balance the number of husbands."

She's making a joke of it, but I can see through it. An enterprising girl like her, I'm sure she'll succeed. She has been sent here today, as I ponder my sins and my fate, by an even larger fate. Something is watching overhead. Something knows everything we've done. Normally I am not a religious person, but sometimes the workings are inescapable.

"I don't think I've ever heard the words 'wild Parsi guy'," I say. "They seem the model of decorum."

"Oh, they're out there, believe me. And if they're out there, I'd find them." She fiddles around with the orange juice. Maybe she's a wine-drinker, and it's past noon but we don't keep it around. Even my husband's nightly beer is stored in the garage. "You asked me what to say. Well, there's too much to say, and not enough. Just say hello from Polly, and if he asks anything more, say I'm in a very stable relationship and he'd be quite proud of – or maybe just surprised by – the way I've turned out. He got me fired from PacBell, by the way, did he ever tell you? He set my feet in an easterly direction. My only regret is there was never time for children. So just say I'm content. Life finds ways of working out, doesn't it? That's probably too much to remember, let alone say."

Is it a question to me? I don't know. Why does she come to me, or am I an unwanted surprise? I think of making lemonade from lemons, something they say that seems a little shallow in its thinking.

"Does it?" I ask. "It seems to me that many lives do not work out as well as yours has. For many reasons, I'm sure."

"Trust me," she says. Then almost immediately, "I must be going. Tell Vivek hello, and I'm sure he'll make the right decision."

She gets into a big car parked in front of our house.

Pramila comes sweeping in from the kitchen to pick up the juice glass. Obviously she's been listening. "What do you suppose that was?" she asks.

"It is what it is," I answer. Another of those clever, hollow sayings.

She tsks-tsks under her breath, and I can imagine her little smirk. "We're running low on fresh fruit," she says. "Next time you go." And when I catch up with her in the kitchen she turns and says, "You should know one thing. If Baba tries to keep me out of Stanford, I'll kill myself. Just sayin'."

This next fruit-run goes uneventfully. Mr. Wally was not out front, arranging the fruit. I ask Sammy, "Where's Wally?" and he smiles but chooses not to answer. So maybe it is eventful. I don't want to ask a second time, or ask a different cousin. I don't want anyone's suspicions confirmed.

DEAR ABHI

I WATCHED HIM this morning juicing a grapefruit, guava, blood orange, mango, plums and grapes and pouring the elixir into a giant glass pitcher. Beads of condensation rolled down the sides, like an ad for California freshness. *Chhoto kaku*, my late father's youngest brother, is vegetarian; the warring juices are the equivalent of eggs and bacon, buttered toast and coffee. He will take tea and toast, but never coffee, which is known to inflame the passions. Life, or the vagaries of the Calcutta marriage market, did not bless him with a wife. Arousal, he believed, would be wasted on him and he has taken traditional measures against it.

Ten years ago this was all farmland, but for the big house and the shingled cottage behind it. No lights spill from the cottage, yet *Chhoto kaku* makes his way across the rocks and cacti to her door. *Don't go*, I breathe, but the door opens. Devorah was alone last night. Usually she comes out around eight o'clock with a mug of coffee and a cigarette, sometimes joined by one of her stay-overs. On our first visit she produced a tray of wild boar sausage that a friend had slaughtered, spiced, cooked and cased, after shooting.

Her hair changes colour. I've seen it green and purple. Today, there are no Mercedes or motorcycles in the yard, she was alone last night. She wears blue jeans and blue work shirts and she smells richly resinous, reminding me of mangoes. Her normal hair is loose and graying.

She told me the day after we'd moved in, "your uncle is a hoot." She calls me Abby, my uncle, Bushy. His name is Kishore Bhushan

Ganguly. We call her Devvie, which in our language approximates the word for goddess. "He looked at my paintings and he said, 'you have the eyes of god.' Isn't that the sweetest thing?" I count myself a man of science, so I must rely on microscopes and telescopes and X-rays to glimpse the world beyond. "He said I see the full range of existence. He said, 'I tremble before you.' Isn't that beautiful?"

When I reported her assessment, Uncle said, "I think she is an advanced soul." I asked how he knew. "She offered me a plate of cold meats. I told her meats inflame the passions." Youngest Uncle is a Brahmin of the old school. "So, she's giving up meats, is that it?" I asked. He said, "I believe so. She said, 'maybe that is my problem.'"

Six months he's been with me, my cherished Youngest Uncle, the bachelor who put me and two cousins through college, married off my sisters and cousins with handsome dowries and set up their husbands, the scoundrels, in business. He delayed, and finally abandoned all hopes of marriage for himself.

When he was an engineer rising through the civil service, then in industry, there'd been the hope of marriage to a neighbour's daughter – beautiful, smart, good family from the right caste and even subcaste. Her father had proposed it and even Oldest Uncle, who approved or vetoed all marriages in the family, declared himself, for once, unopposed. Preparations were started, horoscopes exchanged, a wedding house rented. Her name was Nirmala.

I came home from school one day in my short pants, looking for a servant to make me a glass of fresh lime soda and finding, unimaginably, no one in the kitchen. The servants were all clustered in Oldest Auntie's room joining in the loud lamenting of other pishis and older girl-cousins. I squeezed my own limes then stood on a chair and from the kitchen across a hallway open to the skies, I had a good view into Youngest Uncle's room. He was in tears. He had been betrayed. In those years he was a handsome man in his middle

30's, about my age now, with long, lustrous hair and a thin, clipped moustache. Older Uncle had voided the engagement.

Something unsavory in Nirmala's background had been detected. I heard the word "mishap." Perhaps our family had given her the once-over and found her a little dull, flat chested or older than advertised, or with a lesser dowry. It could have meant a misalignment in the stars, a rumor of non-virginity or suspicion of feeble mindedness somewhere in her family. Or Nirmala might have caught a glimpse of her intended husband and found him too old, too lacking in sex appeal. Every family can relate a similar tale. A promising proposal not taken to its completion is an early sign of the world's duplicity. My parents who married for love and never heard the end of it, did not call it duplicity. They called it not striking while the iron is hot, an image in English I always had difficulty picturing.

In time "Nirmala" stood as a kind of symbol of treacherous beauty. In this case, the rumors bore out. She had a boy on the side, from an unsuitable community. They made a love match, disgracing the name of her good family and rendering her younger sisters unmarriageable to suitable boys. They had two boys before she was eighteen. The sisters scattered to Canada and Australia and had to marry white men. A few years later, Nirmala divorced, and once, I'm told (I had already left for California), she showed up at Youngest Uncle's door, offering her body, begging for money. Proof, as my mother would say, that whatever god decides is for the best. God wished that Youngest Uncle would become middle-aged in the service of lesser-employed brothers and their extended families and that he not spend his sizeable income on a strange woman when it could be squandered on his family instead.

You will see from this I am talking of the not-so-long ago Calcutta, and surmise that I am living, or more properly, was living until a few months ago – with my wife, Sonali, our sons, Vikram and Pramod –

in the Silicon Valley and that my uncle is with us. You would be half-right. My wife kicked me out six months ago. Not so long in calendar days, but in psychological time, eons.

My Christmas bonus eighteen months ago was $250,000. In Indian terms, two and half lakhs of dollars; multiply by forty, a low bank rate, and you come up with ten million rupees: one crore. My father, a middle-class clerk, never made more than two thousand rupees a month and that was only towards the end of his life when the rupee had started to melt. What does it do to a Ballygunge boy, a St. Xavier's boy, to be confronted in half a lifetime with such inflation of expectation, such expansion of the stage upon which we strut and fret? Sonali planned to use the bonus to start a preschool. She was born in California and rarely visits Calcutta, which depresses her. Her parents, retired doctors who were born on the same street as I, live in San Diego.

There are three dozen Indian families in our immediate circle of friends, all of them with children, all of whom share a suspicion that their children's American educational experiences will not replicate the hunger for knowledge and rejection of mediocrity that we knew in less hospitable Indian schools. They would therefore pay anything to replicate some of that nostalgic anxiety, but not the deprivation. She could start a school. Sonali is a fine Montessori teacher. Many of the wives of our friends are teachers. Many of my friends would volunteer to tutor or teach a class. We would have a computer-literate school to do Sunnyvale proud. She spoke to me nightly of dangerous and deprived East Palo Alto where needs are great and the rents are cheap.

If I stay in this country we would have to do it, or something like it. It is a way of recycling good fortune and being part of this model community I've been elected to because of the responsible way I conduct my life. You name it – family values, religious observation, savings, education, voting, tax-paying, PTA, soccer-coaching, nature-hiking, school boards, mowing my lawn, keeping a garden, contributing to charities – I've done it. And in the office: designing, programming, helping the export market and developing patents – I've done that, too. America is a demonstrably better place for my presence. My undistinguished house, bought on a downside market for a mere $675,000 cash, quadrupled in value in the past five years – or more precisely, four of the past five years. It is inconceivable that anything I would do not be a credit to my national origin, my present country and my religious creed.

When something is missing it's not exactly easy to place it. I have given this some thought – I think it is called "evidence of things unseen." Despite external signs of satisfaction, good health, a challenging job, the love and support of family and friends, no depressions or mood swings, no bad habits, I would not call myself happy. I am well-adjusted. We are all extremely well-adjusted. I believe my situation is not uncommon among successful immigrants of my age and background.

I went alone to Calcutta for two weeks, just after the bonus. Sonali didn't go. She took the boys and two of their school friends skiing in Tahoe. She has won medals for her skiing. I am grateful for all those comforts and luxuries but had been feeling unworthy of late. It was Youngest Uncle who had paid for the rigorous Calcutta schools and then for St. Xavier's and that preparation got me the scholarships to IIT and later to Berkeley, but I lacked a graceful way of thanking him. The bonus check was in my wallet. I would be in Calcutta with a crore of rupees in my figurative pocket. I, Abhishek Ganguly of Ballygunge.

Chhoto kaku is now sixty-seven, ten years retired from his post of chemical engineer. The provident funds he'd contributed to for forty years are secure. One need not feel financial concern for Youngest

Uncle, at least in a rupee zone. He has no legal dependents. Everyone into the remotest hinterland of consanguinity has been married. He was living with his two widowed sisters-in-law and their two daughters plus husbands and children in our old Calcutta house. The rent has not been substantially raised since Partition when we arrived from what was then East Bengal and soon to become East Pakistan, then Bangladesh. *Chhoto kaku* was then a boy of eleven. I believe the rent is about fifteen dollars a month, which is reflected in the broken amenities. A man on a bicycle collects the rent on the first of every month. They say he is the landlord's nephew, but the nephew is a frail gentleman of seventy years.

It is strange how one adjusts to the street noise and insects, the power cuts, the Indian-style bathroom, the dust and noise and the single tube of neon light in the living room which casts all nighttime conversations into a harsh pallor and reduces the interior world to an ashen palette of grays and blues. Only for a minute or two do I register Sunnyvale, the mountains, the flowers and garden, the cool breeze, the paintings and rugs and comfortable furniture. And my god, the appliances: our own tandoori oven and a convection oven, the instant hot-tea spout, ice water in the refrigerator door, the tiles imported from Portugal for the floor and countertops. Sonali is an inspired renovator. You would think it was us, the Gangulys of Sunnyvale, who were the long-established and landowning aristocracy and not my uncle who has lived in his single room in that dingy house for longer than I've been on earth.

Youngest Uncle is a small man, moustached, the lustrous long hair nearly gone, fair as we Bengalis go, blessed with good health and a deep voice much admired for singing and for prayer services. He could have acted, or sung professionally. There was talk of sending him to Cambridge in those heady post-Independence years when

England was offering scholarships to identify the likely leaders of its newly liberated possessions. Many of his classmates went, stayed on, and married English girls. He remained in India, citing the needs of his nieces and nephews and aged parents.

The tragedy of his life, if the word is applicable, was having been the last born in the family. He could not marry before his older siblings and they needed his unfettered income to secure their matches. And if he married for his own pleasure the motive would have appeared lascivious. This, he would never do. My father, that striker of, or with, hot irons, had been the only family member to counsel personal happiness over ancestral duty. He called his sisters and other brothers bloodsuckers. When my parents married just after Independence under the spell of Gandhian idealism, they almost regretted the accident that had made their brave and impulsive marriage also appear suitable as to caste and sub-caste. My father would have married a sudra, he said; my mother, a Christian, Parsi, Sikh, or maybe even a Muslim, under proper conditions.

I am always extravagant with gifts for Youngest Uncle. He has all the high-tech goodies my company makes: an e-mail connection and a lightning-fast modem though he never uses it, a cellphone, a scanner, a laser printer, copier, colour television, various tape recorders and stereos. The room cannot accommodate him, electronically speaking, with its single burdened outlet. But the gifts are still in their boxes, carefully dusted, waiting to be given to various grand-nephews still in elementary school. He keeps only the Walkman, on which he plays classic devotional ragas. He's making his spiritual retreat to Varanasi electronically.

I touched his feet in the traditional *pronam*. He touched my shoulder, partially to deflect my gesture, partially to acknowledge it. It is a touch I miss in the States, never giving it and never expecting to receive it. It is a sign that I am home and understood.

"So, *Chhoto kaku*, what's new?" I asked, the invitation for Youngest Uncle to speak about the relatives, the dozens-swollen-to-hundreds of Gangulys who now live in every part of India, and increasingly, the world.

"In Calcutta, nothing is ever new," he said. "In interest of saving money, Rina and her husband, Gautam, are here ..." Rina is the youngest daughter of his next older sister. Thanks to Youngest Uncle's dowry, Rina had got married during the year and brought Gautam to live in her house, an unusual occurrence, although nothing is as it was in India, even in polite, conservative, what used to be called *bhadralok*, Bengali society.

"Where do they stay, uncle?"

"In this room."

There are no other spare rooms. It is a small house.

"They are waiting for me to die. They expect me to move in with Sukhla-pishi."

That would be his oldest sister-in-law, the one we call Front Room Auntie for her position at the window that overlooks the street. She is over eighty. Nothing happens on Rash Behari Avenue that she doesn't know. The rumor, deriving from those first post-Partition years, is she had driven *Anil-kaku*, her young husband, my oldest uncle, mad. He'd died of something suspicious which was officially a burst appendix. Something burst, that is true. Disappointment, rage, failure of his schemes, who can say? It is Calcutta. He was a civil engineer and had been offered a position outside of Ballygunge in a different part of the city, but rather than leave the house and neighborhood, Sukhla-pishi had taken to her bed in order to die. (I should add that modern science sheds much light on intractable behavior. Sukhla-pishi is obviously agoraphobic; a pill would save us all much heartache.) *Anil-kaku* turned down the job and she climbed out of bed and took her seat on the windowsill. All of that happened before I was born. There had been no children – they were then in their middle-twenties – so she became the first of Youngest Uncles' lifelong obligations.

"This is your house, uncle," I said. "Don't be giving up your rights." As if he hadn't already surrendered everything.

"Rights were given long ago. Her mother holds the lease."

I should say a few words about my cousin-sister Rina. She is most unfortunate to look at, or to be around. I was astonished that she'd found any boy to marry, thinking anyone so foolish would be like her, a flawed appendage to a decent family. We'd been most pleasantly wrong. He was handsome, which goes a long way in our society, a dashing, athletic flight steward with one of the new private airlines that fly between Calcutta and the interior of eastern India. We understood he was in management training. Part of the pre-marriage negotiation was the best room in the house, that would allow him to pocket his housing allowance from the airline while subletting the company flat, and his own car, computer, television, stereo, printer and tape recorder. He'd scouted the room before marriage since the demands were not only generic, but included brand names and serial numbers.

"I cannot say more, they are listening," said my uncle.

It was then that I noticed the new furnishings in the room, a calendar on the wall from Gautam's employer. This wasn't Youngest Uncle's room anymore, though he'd lived in it for over fifty years. He'd sobbed over Nirmala on that bed. The move to the sunny, dusty, noisy front room, rolling a thin mattress on Sukhla-pishi's floor, had already been made. Next would be Gautam's selling on the black market of all the carefully boxed, unopened electronics I'd smuggled in.

"Let us go for tea," I suggested, putting my hand on his arm, noting its tremble and sponginess. I kept an overseas membership in the Tollygunge Club for moments like this, prying favourite relatives away from family scrutiny, letting them drink Scotch or a beer free of disapproval, but he wouldn't budge.

"They won't permit it," he said. "I've been told not to leave the house."

"They? Who's they?"

"The boy, the girl. Her."

"Rina? You know Rina, uncle, she's – " I wanted to say "flawed." On past visits I'd contemplated taking her out to the Tolly for a stiff gin just to see if there was a different Rina, waiting to be released. " – Harmless."

"Her mother," he whispered. "And the boy."

I heard precipitous noises outside the door. "Babu?" came my aunt's query, "what is going on in my daughter's room?"

"We are talking, pishi," I said. "We'll be just out."

"Rina doesn't want you in there. She will be taking her bath."

The shower arrangement was in uncle's room. His books, the only ones in the house, lined the walls but Rina's saris and Gautam's suits filled the cupboard. It was the darkest, coolest, quietest, largest and only fully serviced room in the house. Not for the first time did it occur to me that poverty corrupts everyone in India, just as wealth does the same in America. Nor did family life – so often evoked as the glue of Indian society, evidence of superiority over Western selfishness and rampant individualism – escape its collateral accounting as the source of all horrors. I suggested we drop in at the Tolly for a whiskey or two.

"I cannot leave the house," he said. "I am being watched. I will be reported."

"Watched for what?"

"Gautam says that I have cheated on my taxes. The CBI is watching me twenty-four hours a day from their cars and from across the street. I must turn over everything to him to clear my name."

"Kaku! You are the most honest man I have ever met."

"No man leads a blameless life."

"Gautam's a scoundrel. When he's finished draining your accounts, he'll throw you in the gutter."

"They are watching you too, Abhi, for all the gifts you have given. Gautam says you have defrauded the country. We are worse than agents of the Foreign Hand. He has put you on record, too."

All those serial numbers, of course – and I thought he was merely a thief. Every time I have given serious thought to returning to India for retirement or even earlier, perhaps to give my children more direction and save them from the insipidness of an American life, I am brought face to face with villainies, hypocrisies, that leave me speechless. Elevator operators collecting fares. Clerks demanding bribes, not to forgive charges, but to accept payments and stamp "paid" on a receipt. Rina and Gautam follow a pattern. I don't want to die in America, but India makes it so hard, even for its successful runaways.

And so the idea came to me that this house in which I'd spent the best years of my childhood, the house that the extended Ganguly clan of East Bengal had been renting for over fifty years, had to be available for the right price if I could track down the owner in the three days remaining on my visit. It was one of the last remaining single-family, one-story bungalows on a wide, maidan-split boulevard lined with expensive apartment blocks. I, Abhishek Ganguly, would become owner of a house on Rash Behari Avenue, Ballygunge, paid for from the check in my pocket and my first order of business would be to expel those slimy schemers, Gautam and Rina and her mother, and any other relative who stood in the way. Front Room-pishi could stay.

Perhaps I oversold the charms of California. I certainly oversold the enthusiasm my dear wife might feel for housing an uncle she'd never met. Rina and Gautam would not leave voluntarily. Auntie would cause a fight. There'd be cursing, wailing, threats, denunciations. Nothing a few well distributed gifts could not settle. Come back with me for six months of good food and sunshine, I said, no CBI surveillance, and you can return to a clean house and your own room, dear Youngest Uncle.

Bicycle-nephew was more than happy to trade a monthly eight hundred rupees for ten million, cash. And with India being a land of miracles and immediate transformation as well as timeless inertia, I returned to California feeling like a god in the company of my liberated *Chhoto kaku*, owner, *zamindar* if you will, like my ancestors in pre-Partition East Bengal, of property, preserver of virtue and expeller of evil.

It is America, contrary to received opinion, which resists cataclysmic self-reinvention. In my two-week absence, my dear wife had engaged an architect to transform a boarded-over, five-shop strip mall in East Palo Alto into plans for the New Athens Academy, the Agora of Learning. Where weeds now push through the broken slabs of concrete, there will be fountains and elaborate gardens. Each class will plant flowers and vegetables in February and harvest in May. Classes will circulate through the plots. I can picture toga-clad teachers. New Athens will incorporate the best of East and West, Tagore's Shantiniketan and Montessori's Rome, Confucius and Dewey, sports and science, classics and computers, all fueled by Silicon Valley resources. She'd started enrolling children for two years hence.

And then I had to inform her – that outpost of Vesuvius – that my one-crore bonus cheques now rested in the account of one Atulya Ghosh, the very cool, twenty-year-old grandson of Bicycle Ghosh, nephew of old Landlord Ghosh, the presumably late owner.

One of the Ghoshes, it might have been Atulya's grandfather, had been the rumored lover of a pishi of mine who'd been forced to leave the house in disgrace. She killed herself, in fact. Young Ray-Bans Ghosh was a Toronto-based greaser, decked out in filmi-filmi Bollywood sunglasses and a stylish scarf, forked over a throbbing motorcycle – all I could ask for as an on-site enforcer. He took my money and promised there'd be no problems: he had friends. Rina, Gautam, and Rina's mother deserved to share the pokey company flat bordering a paddy field on the outskirts of Cossipore.

Sonali wailed, she broke down in tears, sobbing, "New Athens, New Athens!" she cried. "My Agora, my Agora! All my dreams, all my training!" What had I been thinking? And the answer was, amazingly, she was right. I hadn't thought about her or the school, at all.

"You don't care about me. You're always complaining about our boys' education, you think I'm lazy, you only care about your goddamn family in goddamn Calcutta ..."

"I should return home," said *Chhoto kaku.*

"Oh, no," she cried. "*I* should return home! And I'm going to!"

She stood at the base of the stairway – I could rhapsodize over the marble, the recessed lighting under the handrail, the paintings and photographs lining the stairwell, but that is from a lifetime ago. And her beauty, I am easily inflamed. I admit it, and I will never see a more beautiful woman than Sonali, even as she threw plates at my head. "Boys! Pramod, Vikram! Pack your bags immediately. We're leaving for San Diego!"

Chhoto kaku began to cry. I held him. Sonali went upstairs to organize the late-night getaway. The boys struggled to pack their video games and computers. The ever-enticing, ever-dangerous phenomenon of the HAP, the Hindu-American Princess, had been described to me by friends who'd urged me not to marry here, but to go back to India. Do not take on risky adventures with the second-generation daughters of American entitlement. Did I listen? Did she love me for my money, had she ever loved me? Was this all a dream? I sat on the bottom step, hiding my tears, cradling my eyes and forehead against my bent arm, while *Chhoto kaku* ran his fingers through my hair and sang to me, very low and soft, a prayer I recognized from a lifetime ago.

Well, enough of that. Justice is swift and mercy unavailing. The property split left Sonali and the boys in the big house and my uncle and me in this tiny rental. Last Christmas there was no bonus. My boss, Nitin Mehta, called me aside and said, "bad times are coming, Abhi. We have to stay ahead of the wave. I want you to cut twenty percent of your tech group." So I slashed, I burned. Into the fire went everyone with an H-1B visa; back to Bombay with Lata Deshpande who was getting married in a month. Off to a taxi in Oakland went Yuri, who'd come overnight from Kazakhstan to Silicon Valley, thinking it a miracle. This Christmas there will be no job, even for me. Impulse breeds disaster, I've been taught.

In a month or two we'll be free to move back to Calcutta. Ray-Bans Ghosh informs me the "infestation" has been routed. But Youngest Uncle has found a girlfriend in America. Kaku and the Goddess; my walls glow with her paintings. The turpentine smell of mango haunts the night.

In the summer of my fourteenth year, Youngest Uncle was given a vacation cottage in Chota Nagpur, a forest area on the border of Bihar and West Bengal. Ten members of the family went in May when the heat and humidity in Calcutta both reached triple digits. The cottage was shaded by a grove of mango trees too tall to climb. Snakes and birds and rats and clouds of insects gorged on the broken fruit. The same odour of rotting mango envelops the Goddess and the sharp tang of her welcome.

She is a well-known painter in the Bay Area and represented in New York. The first time we visited, Youngest Uncle said, "You smell of mango," and she'd reached out and touched him. "Oh, sweeties," she said, "it's just the linseed oil." She never seems to cook. On garbage collection days there is nothing outside her door yet she can produce cold platters of the strangest foods. She has an inordinate number of overnight guests who doubtless return to their city existence, trailing mango fumes. My uncle brings her sweet lassi, crushed ice in sweetened yoghurt, lightly laced with mango juice. I hope that in place of a heart she does not harbor a giant stone.

That summer in Choto Nagpur, I had a girlfriend. There was another cabin not so distant where another Calcutta family had brought their daughter for the high-summer school holidays. We had seen each other independent of parental authority, meaning we had passed one another on the main street of the nearest village, and our eyes had met – in my twenty-four years' memory I want to say "locked" – but neither of us paused or acknowledged the other's presence. The fact that she didn't exactly ignore me meant I now had a girlfriend, a face to focus on and something to boast about when school resumed and the monsoons marooned us. I had the next thing to a wife, a Nirmala of my own. Knowing her name and her parents' address in Calcutta and trusting that she was out there waiting for me when the time would come, I was able to put the anxieties of marriage aside for the next five years.

When I was eighteen I asked Youngest Uncle to launch a marriage inquiry. I provided her father's name and address – I'd even walked by their house on the way to school in hopes of seeing her again and perhaps locking eyes in confirmation. Youngest Uncle was happy to do so. He reported her parents to be charming and cultured people with a pious outlook, whose ancestral origins in Bangladesh lay in an adjoining village to our own. Truly an adornment to our family. It seemed that the girl in question, however, whose name by now I've quite forgotten, was settled in a place called Maryland-America and had two lovely children. And so, outwardly crushed but partially relieved, I took the scholarship to IIT and then to Berkeley, met Sonali at a campus mixer thrown by outgoing Indo-Americans for nervous Indians, had my two lovely children, made millions and lost it and the rest is history, or maybe not.

All of my life, good times and bad, rich and poor, married and alone, I have read the Gita and tried to be guided by its immortal wisdom. It teaches our life – this life – is but a speck on a vast spectrum, but our ears are less reliable than a dog's, a dolphin's or a bat's, our eyes less than a bird's in comprehending it. I have understood it in terms of science, the heavy elements necessary to life, the calcium, phosphorous, iron and zinc, settle on us from exploded stars. We are entwined in the vast cycle of creation and destruction; the spark of life is inextinguishable. Today human, but who knows about tomorrow? We are the fruit and the rot that infects it, the mango and the worm.

Ray-Bans Ghosh now wants to put his crore of rupees to work in Toronto. Dear Abhi-babu, he writes, tear down this useless old house, put up luxury condos and you'll be minting money. Front Room pishi, who misses nothing outside the window, reports that she has seen evil Gautam in various disguises sneaking about the property. Dear Abhi, she pleads, come back, that man will kill me if he can and your cousin Rina and her mother will bury me in the yard like a Christian or worse, and please send my love to *Chhoto kaku* and your lovely wife and children, whom I've still not met.

Perhaps my Nirmala waits for me in Calcutta, perhaps in Tokyo or Maryland or the ancestral village in Bangladesh. Youngest Uncle will stay here just a while longer, if he may, keeping my house clean and ready for whatever God plans. He has bought himself some brushes and watercolors, and takes his instruction from the Goddess who guides his hand and trains him to see, he says, at last. His old middle room has been vacant these past several months. It will suit me.

This life, which I understood once in terms of science – the heavy elements, the calcium, phosphorous, iron, and zinc, settled on us from exploded stars – is but one of an infinity of lives. The city, the world, has come and gone an infinite number of times. One day I expect my Nirmala, whatever her name, to come to my door wherever that door will be, our eyes will lock, and I will invite her in.

BREWING TEA IN THE DARK

MY YOUNGEST UNCLE and I and a busload of other English-speakers were on a tour of Tuscany, leaving Florence at dawn, then on to Siena, followed by a mountain village, a farm lunch, another mountain village, the Leaning Tower of Pisa, and back to Florence after dark. I had planned to spread his ashes unobtrusively over a peaceful patch of sloping land, but each stop seemed more appealing than the one before, and so by lunchtime I was still holding on to the urn.

The mountain towns on our morning stops had been seductive. I could imagine myself living in any of them, walking the steep streets and taking my dinners in sidewalk cafés. I could learn Italian, which didn't seem too demanding. The fresh air and Mediterranean Diet could add years to my life.

The countryside of Tuscany in no way resembles the red-soil greenery of Bengal. Florence does not bring Kolkata to mind, except in its jammed sidewalks. My uncle wanted to live his next life as an Italian or perhaps as some sort of creature in Italy, maybe just as a tall, straight cypress (this is a theological dispute; life might be eternal, but is a human life guaranteed every rebirth?). Each time that he and his lady friend, Devvie, a painter, returned from Italy to California he pronounced himself more Italian than ever, a shrewd assessor of fine art and engineering, with a new hat, shoulder bag, jacket or scarf to prove it. He said Devvie was the prism through which the white light of his adoration was splintered into all the colors of the universe. (It sounds more natural in Bangla, our language). If that is true, many men are daubed in her colors. She taught him the Tuscan palette, the umbers and sienas.

At the farm lunch a woman of my approximate age – whose gray curls were bound in a kind of ringletted ponytail – sat opposite me at one of the refectory tables. She was wearing a dark blue "University of Firenze" sweatshirt over faded blue jeans. In the lissome way she moved, and in the way she dressed, she seemed almost childlike. I am forty-five, but slow and heavy in spirit.

She dropped her voice to a whisper. "I can't help noticing that urn you're carrying. Is it what I ..."

I had placed it unobtrusively, I'd thought, on the table between the wine glasses. It was stoppered and guaranteed airtight, a kind of Thermos bottle of ashes. I was afraid that if I put him on the floor an errant foot might touch him.

"Very perceptive," I said. "It's my uncle."

"Lovely to meet you, sir," she said to the urn. Then to me, "You can call me Rose." *Call me Rose?* I must have squinted, but she said, "You were talking to him back in Siena. You were sitting on a bench and holding it in your lap and I heard you. Of course, I couldn't understand what you were saying, but I'd never seen anything like it."

"Why the mystery about your name?" I asked.

"You'll find out," she said. Perhaps she changed her name every day, or on every trip, or for every man she met. I told her my name, Abhi, short for Abhishek.

The farm landscape reminded me of paintings on the walls of Italian restaurants: mounded vineyards framed by cypress trees, against a wall of purple hills sprinkled with distant, whitewashed villas. She moved like a dancer to the fence, then turned, and called to me.

"Why not right here?"

I walked over to the fence, but a goat wandered up to us, looking for food, and tried to butt me through the slats. Then he launched a flurry of shiny black pellets.

"Maybe not," she said.

When we remounted the tour bus, the aisle seat next to me turned up vacant. "May I?" she asked. She told me that my morning seatmate had also made a connection with the urn and a possible bomb, or shortwave radio. He too had seen me talking in a strange language in Siena, probably Arabic.

During the next leg of the trip, she opened up to me: "You came here on a mission. So did I, in a way. I read that an old friend of mine was going to be in Florence for a Renaissance music festival. He plays the mandolin. And suddenly I wanted to see him again. Not to be with him – goodness, he has a wife and family – but I thought how funny it would be if we just happened to run into each other."

I could not have imagined so much disclosure in a single outburst. I couldn't even understand her motivation. Funny? The impulsiveness of my fellow Americans is often mysterious to me, but I listened with admiration. We'd never met and we were on a bus in Tuscany, but she was spilling her secrets. Or did she consider me a harmless sounding post? Or did she have no secrets? And then I wondered had she – like me – been pried open by some recent experience? Perhaps our normal defenses had been weakened.

"Maybe you had a wake-up call," I said. The things we do that elude all reason, because suddenly, we have to do them.

She seemed to ponder the possibility, then consigned it to a secret space for future negotiation. After a few moments she asked, "Where are you from?"

Always an ambiguous question: where are you really from? India? Am I from Kolkata? California? Bay Area? She said, "I work in a library in a small town in Massachusetts, two blocks from Emily Dickinson's house."

She'd been married, but not to her mandolinist. She'd gone to New York to dance, she married, but she'd injured herself and turned to painting, and then she'd divorced and started writing. By her estimation she was a minor, but not a failed, writer. Like most Bangla-speakers of my generation, I've known a number of poets and writers, although most were employed in more mundane endeavors, by day. I had never considered them minor, or failed.

And then her narrative, or her confessions, stopped and I felt strangely bereft. I sensed she was waiting for me to reciprocate. What did I have to match her?

"Are you married?" she asked.

I began to understand that something thicker was in the air. "Why do you ask?"

"You have an appealing air," she said.

It is my experience in the West that Indian men, afraid to press their opinions or exert their presence, are often perceived as soulful. Many's the time I've wanted to say, to very well-meaning ladies, just because I have long, delicate fingers and large, deep-brown eyes and a mop of black, unruly hair, do not ascribe to me greater sensitivity, sensuality, or innocence, or some kind of unthreatening, prefeminist manliness. Our attempts to accommodate a new culture are often interpreted as clumsy, if forgivable. I think my uncle and his painter friend enjoyed such a relationship, based on mutual misreading, but in his case all of the clichés might have been true. He was, truly, an innocent. Unlike him, I have no trouble saying "fuck" in mixed company.

"Do you have children?" she persisted.

I have a girl and a boy, who stay with their mother and her parents in San Diego. In my world, the love of one's family is the only measure of success, and in that aspect, I have failed. I said only, "yes."

"I'm sorry," she said. "It's none of my business."

My uncle was an afflicted man. He never married. His income paid for the education of all the boys in the family, and the dowries of all the girls. In a place where family means everything, and if part of the family is pure evil, even one's house can be a prison. Literally, a prison: he lived in a back bedroom, afraid even to be seen from the street. He was forced to pay his grandniece's husband ten thousand rupees a month, on the threat of his turning over certain documents to the CBI that would prove something. You ask why he didn't protect himself, why he didn't sue, why his passivity was allowed to confirm the most heinous charges? And I say, Indian "justice" is too slow and corrupt. Cases linger before judges awaiting their bribes. Cases go on as lawyers change sides, as they win stay after stay.

That grim prison was the house of my fondest memories, the big family compound on Rash Behari Avenue that our family began renting the moment of their arrival from the eastern provinces, now known as Bangladesh. Our neighborhood was an east Bengal enclave. We grew up still speaking the eastern dialect. We thought of ourselves as refugees, even the generation, like my grandparents', which had arrived before Partition. In soccer, we still supported East Bengal against the more-established Calcutta team, Mohun Bagan. It's the most spirited competition in all of sports, perhaps in the world.

Six years ago, I'd arrived for my annual visit, this time with a quarter-million dollars in year-end bonus money. It was the dot. com era nearing its end – although we thought it would go on forever – and I had been a partner in a start-up. When my uncle spilled out his story, and I could see the evidence all around me, I also had the solution in my pocket. I acted without thinking. No courts, no police, no unseemly newspaper coverage that would tarnish the family name. I simply bought the house and kicked the vermin out. But I had forgotten that my wife had a use for that money; a school she'd planned to start. I came back from Kolkata with my uncle in tow. She and the children left for San Diego a week later.

She slept on the long ride to Pisa. She slept like a child, no deep breathing, no snoring. I wished she'd turned her head towards me. I would have held her, even embraced her. It was the first time in years that I'd felt such a surge of protectiveness.

There is very little good I can say about Pisa. I'm of two minds about the Leaning Tower. It is iconic, but ugly. It's a monument to phenomenal incompetence, and now the world is invested in a medieval mistake. Actually, I'm not of two minds. It is an abomination. Preserving the mistake is a crime against the great Italian tradition of engineering. In the wide lawns around the Tower, various bands of young tourists, mostly Japanese, posed with their arms outstretched, aligning them for photos in a way to suggest they were holding up the crippled Tower.

We walked towards the Tower, past stalls of souvenir-sellers, most of them, if not all, Bangladeshi, hawking Leaning Tower T-shirts and kitchen towels. They called out to us in English, but I could hear them muttering among themselves in Bangla, "It's an older bunch. Put out the fancy stuff."

I stopped by, drawn in by the language. We may be one of the pioneering languages of Silicon Valley, but we are also the language of the night, the cooks and dishwashers and hole-in-the-wall restaurants and cheap clothing stalls around the world. Then they studied me a little closer. "Hey, brother!" This came in Bangla. "Something nice for your girlfriend?" They held up white T-shirts, stamped with the Leaning Tower.

"What kind of gift is that?" I answered back. "She'd have to lean like a cripple to make it straight."

They invited me behind the stalls. Rose came closer, but stayed on the edge of the sidewalk. I felt a little guilty – this was my call from the unconscious, the language-hook. I remembered my uncle, who had brought his devotional tapes to California, and many evenings I would return from work and the lights would be off, and he would be singing to his Hemanta Mukherjee tapes, and I would keep the lights off and brew tea in the dark.

Behind the display bins, the men had stored trunks and trunks of trinkets and T-shirts and towels and tunics, nearly all of them Pisa-related. On each trunk, in Bangla, they had chalked the names of cities: Pisa, Florence, Rome, Venice and Pompeii.

The three stall-owners were cousins. They introduced themselves: Wahid, Hesham and Ali, cousins from a village a kilometer from my grandparents' birthplace. They knew the town well, and the big house that had been ours, the zamindari house, the Hindu's house. Maybe their grandfathers, as small children, had worked there, or maybe they had just stolen bananas from the plantation.

"Then you are from the Ganguly family?" they asked me, and I nodded, bowing slightly, "Abhishek Ganguly." Hindu, even Brahmin: opposite sides of a one-kilometer world.

The buried, collective memory forever astonishes. Nothing in the old country could have brought our families together, yet here we were in the shadow of the Leaning Tower of Pisa, remembering the lakes and rivers, the banana plantation, my great-grandfather's throwing open his house on every Hindu and Muslim feast-day. In the olden days, in the golden east of Bengal where all our poetry originated, the Hindus had the wealth, the Muslims had the numbers, and both were united against the British.

My ancestral residence (which I've never seen; after Partition, my parents even tore up the old photos they'd carried with them), I learned, is now a school. The banana plantation is now a soccer field and cricket pitch. Wahid, Hesham, and Ali, and three remoter cousins – what we call "cousin-brothers", which covers any degree of relatedness including husbands of cousins' sisters – have a lorry, and when the tourist season is over in Pisa they will strike their stalls and go to Florence and sell Statue of David kitsch, or to Venice and sell gondola kitsch. In the winter they will go to southern Spain and sell Alhambra kitsch.

But think of the distance these cheap but still over-priced T-shirts have traveled! Uzbek cotton, spun in Cambodia, stamped in China and sent to a middleman somewhere in the Emirates, to be distributed throughout Europe, matching the proper Western icon to the right city and the proper, pre-paid sellers. For one month they will return to Bangladesh, bringing gifts to their children and parents, and doubtless, enlarging their families.

The cousins had come to Italy four years ago, starting out by spreading blankets on the footpaths and selling China-made toys. Now they have transportable stalls and in a couple of years the six cousins will pool their money and buy a proper store, somewhere, and bring their wives and children over. Right now, they send half of their earnings back to their village, where the wives have built solid houses and the children are going to English-medium schools and want to become doctors and teachers. Their wives have opened up tea-stalls and stitching-shops. "We are Bengalis first, then Hindu or Muslim after," said Wahid, perhaps for my benefit. "If anyone says he is first a Muslim or a Hindu, I give him wide berth. He has a right to his beliefs, but I do not share them."

All of this I translated for my girlfriend, Rose. Then we sat at a sidewalk café and drank a glass of white wine, looking out on the Tower and the ant-sized climbers working their way up the sides, waving from the balconies. I was happy.

"I think you're a little too harsh on the Tower," she said.

We reached Florence in the dark. There seemed little question that we would spend the night together, in her hotel or mine. Outside the bus-park only one food stall was still open. I bought apples and a bottle of wine. The young man running it did all his calculations in Italian, until I stopped him, in Bangla. "That's a lot of *taka*, isn't it?" and the effect was of a puppet master jerking a doll's strings. He mentioned the name of his village, this one far, far in the east, near Chittagong, practically in Burma. His accent was difficult for me, as was mine to him. "Bangla is the international language of struggle," he said.

The unexpected immersion in Bengal had restored a certain confidence. It was the last thing, or the second-last thing, I'd expected from a trip into the wilds of Tuscany. I was swinging the plastic sack of wine and apples, with the urn tucked under my arm, and Rose said, "Let me take the urn." I lifted my arm slightly, and she reached in.

"Oops," she said.

My religion holds that the body is sheddable, but the soul is eternal. My uncle's soul still exists, despite the cremation. It has time to find a new home, entering through the soft spot in a newborn's skull. I felt he was still with me, there in Italy, but perhaps he'd remained back in California. The soul is in the ether, like a particle in the quanta; it can be in California one second, and Kolkata the next. But he'd wanted to find an Italian home, and now his matter lay in a dusty, somewhat oily mass on the cobblestones of Florence, amid shards of glass and ceramic. It will join some sort of Italian flux. It will be picked up on the soles of shoes, it will flow in the gutter, it will be devoured by flies and picked over by pigeons. If I am truly a believer in our ancient traditions, then it doesn't matter where he lies like a clot of mud while his soul still circles, awaiting its new house, wherever that house might be.

"It's all right," I said. In fact, a burden had been lifted.

Her hotel was near at hand. This was an event I had not planned. It had been three years since any sexual activity, and that had been brief and not consoling. In the slow-rising elevator, she squeezed my hand. Sex with a gray-haired lady, however slim and girlish, lay outside my fantasy. How to behave, what is the etiquette? She'd taken off her glasses, and she was humming something wordless. Under her University of Firenze sweatshirt, I could make out only the faintest mounds, the slightest crease. Even in the elevator's harsh fluorescent light, I saw no wrinkles in her face.

As we walked down the corridor, she slipped me her key-card. My fingers were trembling. It took three stabs to open the door. The moment the door was shut, and a light turned on, she walked to the foot of the bed, and turned to face me. The bedspread was a bright, passionate red. It was an eternal moment: the woman's smile, her hands closing around the ends of her sweatshirt, and then beginning to pull it up. I dropped the bag of wine and apples. So this is how it plays, this is how people like us do it. Her head disappeared briefly under the sweater, and then she tossed the University of Firenze aside on the red bedspread and she stood before me, a thin woman with small breasts, no bra, and what appeared to be a pink string looped against her side.

"Now you know," she said, and began kissing me madly. "Come to my bed of crimson joy."

What I knew was this: she was bald. Her wig had been caught in the sleeve of her sweater. The pink string was a fresh scar down her ribcage, then curling up between her breasts. But we were on the bed and my hands were over her scalp, then on her breasts and the buttons of her jeans, and her fingers were on my belt and pants.

There is much to respect in this surrender to passion. After sex, there is humor, and honesty. I poured the wine and she retired to the bathroom, only to reappear in her red "Shirley MacLaine" wig. With her obviously unnatural, burgundy-colored hair, there's a flash of sauciness atop her comely face and body. And so passion arose once again. "I've got more," she said. There was a black "Liza Minelli," and a blonde.

When we sipped the wine, she told me she'd been given a year, maybe two. But who knows, in this world miracles have been known to happen.

It is overwhelming, the first vision of The David, standing a ghostly white at the end of a long, sculpture-lined hall. An adoring crowd surrounds him, whatever the hour or the day. Viewed from afar, in profile, he is a haughty, even arrogant figure. His head is turned. He is staring at his immediate enemy, Goliath.

"That pose is called contrapposto," Rose whispered. She was wearing her red Shirley MacLaine wig, and she looked like a slightly wicked college woman. David's weight is supported on the right leg – the left leg is slightly raised – but the right arm is lank, and his curled hand cradles a smooth stone. The left arm is bent, and the biceps bunched. The leather sling lies on his shoulder and slithers down his back. Yet when I stood at his side, looking up directly into his eyes, the haughtiness disappeared. I read doubt, maybe fear. It's as though Michelangelo were looking into David's future, beyond the immediate victory. If I remember my Christian schooling, David would go on to become a great king and poet, the founder of a dynasty leading eventually to Jesus Christ, but he will lose his beloved son Absalom in a popular uprising against him and he will send a loyal general to his death in order to possess his wife. In the end, for all his heroism, he will grow corrupt in his pride and arrogance; his is a tattered regime. All of this I felt at that moment, and tried to communicate.

There is so much tragedy in his eyes. He knows he will accomplish this one great thing in the next few minutes, but regret will flow for the rest of his life. David is a monument to physical perfection, the antidote to the Leaning Tower.

And what about us? I wonder. She took my arm as we walked down the swarming sidewalk outside the Accademia. We passed through a great open square, near the Uffizi Palace. Crews were setting up folding chairs for an evening concert of Renaissance music.

"Will you come with me?" she asked.

Of course I would. I would see her mandolinist. We would get there early and sit in the front row. I would stand behind her after the concert, assuming she could make her way to the stage against the press of admirers, and she would ask him, "remember me?"

Maybe she would wear her gray ponytail wig. He would be more comfortable with that, more likely to remember her. In some way, I would learn more about her. "*Oh, Rose!*" he might exclaim. Or he might dismiss her with a flick of his fingers.

"If I'm still above ground next year, and if I came to your house, would you welcome me in?"

And I can only say, "I will open the door."

THE QUALITY OF LIFE

1. **I WAS IN THE HOTEL BATHROOM**, brushing and flossing, with CNN on loud. *"We'll call this another story about undocumented aliens in south Texas. But a story with a twist."* Undocumented aliens get my attention. South Texas doesn't, much.

"Every week, Jacinto Juarez, known in this hot and humid corner of southeast Texas as JJ, and his son, Junior, known as Three-J, do what responsible farmers always do: take a tour of the property, check and mend the fences, inspect the livestock, take moisture readings and measure the growth of crops. Since they know every square inch of their two hundred and forty acres, some thirty-five miles southwest of Corpus Christi, they also check for the little things. And two weeks ago, JJ and Three-J noticed a very significant little thing: *this*."

That brought me out from the bathroom. *This* appeared to be a large hole in a small bluff.

"JJ's property dips down to San Fernando Creek but the rich bottomlands are soft, not easily inspected. So, he planted some trees and even a stand of bamboo, and tended to leave it alone. But two weeks ago, right here, he noticed a recently excavated burrow, leading out to what he calls his private 'wetland'."

Mr. Juarez took over. "This here crick empties into a big estuary, then into Corpus Harbor. Just about any animal in the world could be hitching a ride on a tanker and if they jump ship there's no way they're leaving. My granddaddy used to organize jaguar hunts out here. I've seen more coyotes than I can count, and armadillos and javalinos by the thousands, but I never seen a burrow like this."

"I set a trapline around it," said Three-J, "and I baited it with some real smelly rabbit. Got a coyote pup about three hundred yards downstream, but it didn't come out of that burrow."

"So," CNN broke in, "JJ borrowed a night-vision camera. It took two weeks, and he's finally got his answer. But it's an answer that leaves us with a bigger question. Barring the possibility of its being an escaped exotic pet, or being fattened for a feast, did this mystery guest hitch a ride on an oil tanker from Venezuela – or did he make it all the way on his, or, I should say, on *her* own? Or is this another instance of global warming pushing fauna out of ancestral environments and forcing them north?"

And then, through the green, vaguely fluoroscopic footage of night vision goggles we watched the emergence of something truly new on our continent: a hundred and fifty pounds of aquatically adapted rodent, a pot-bellied pig-sized South American capybara, an immensely inflated guinea pig with slick hair and long skinny legs.

"Say hello to Cappy. And goodbye. Not knowing the nature of the beast, Jacinto Juarez instinctively reacted as a farmer, and shot it. In its native Venezuelan habitat, capybaras are ravenous browsers. Failure to find suitable grasses and aquatic plants might well drive him – or in Cappy's case, her – to pillage beans and corn. Doctors at the University of Texas-Brownsville who performed the necropsy confirmed that Cappy was pregnant with three near-full term offspring. She had been impregnated five months ago. Tonight in these lonely Texas barrens, there might be a male capybara searching wetlands for a mate."

I returned to the bathroom, sick with a kind of empathy. To die in such a way, in such a place, after the great adventure of her life: oh, Mother!

2. This starts in cool and leafy Bangalore, a town where many trinkets of Empire have run their course. Long before the things we read about today, Bangalore was just a dowdy old army cantonment, the base of the Southern Command of the British, and then the Indian Army.

Bangalore's boulevards are wide enough to channel military parades, caissons, battle camels and ornamental elephants. It's a pleasantly situated, high altitude town of year-round salubriousness – dry in the monsoons, cool in the summer, warm in the winter, devoid of mosquitoes – sprinkled with parks, golf courses, military academies, imposing administrative buildings of red and yellow sandstone, and in the old days, whites-only clubs with cheap liquor. Its sole international raison d'être had to do with the British Army. Even after Independence, Bangalore did not destroy its Victoria statues.

Back in the 1870s, my enterprising great-great-grandfather, Mohan Nilingappa, recently arrived in Bangalore from our ancestral village up north, purchased a spacious bungalow, "Primrose Estate", from a departing Englishman who'd lost his family in an epidemic. It was situated in an outlying community called Murphy Town. Anticipating a large family, Mohan added a north and south wing. "Primrose Estate" became "Nilingappa Bhavan."

Nilingappa gospel has it that my g-g-grandfather never suffered a single humiliation at the hands of our colonial masters; was never mocked or excluded for his faith, his accent, or the color of his skin. Obviously, the Nilingappas, even in the 1870s, were so worthy that they alone, among the hundreds of millions of Indian subjects, avoided the abuse – official, and ad hoc – of colonial arrogance. My father loved the British. He'd studied in Edinburgh and he wore his pre-War Scottish tweeds right up to the minute of his death.

I doubt that the British have ever been capable of extending equal treatment to Indians. At most, the early Nilingappas might have profited from a certain indulgence for one simple reason: they were brewers. An army might march on its stomach, but it fights on its liquor, and Mohan Nilingappa held the purveyors' license to the cantonment.

During the Raj, satellite communities like Fraser Town and Murphy Town ringed the city. The old officer corps – the various Frasers and Murphys – built splendid residences behind high stucco walls. Christian hospitals, white clubs and Anglican churches followed. The Bangalore climate encouraged English-style gardening; hence, their horticultural societies and garden tours. Some of the retirees even stayed on in their cool and shaded bungalows and married young or recently widowed Indian and Anglo-Indian women. There was no reason to go back to England so long as loyal servants, English-trained cooks, golf foursomes and cheap liquor were easily requisitioned, and thanks to their off-colour wives and children, they couldn't go back anyway.

Then came the great, unthinkable calamity. Independence. The majority of active-duty British officers sold their modest mansions to Indian professionals in the great exodus of 1947. My father had grown up as part of the only Indian family in a British neighborhood; all the neighbors I remember from the early 1960s were totally Indian. Murphy Town and Fraser Town were already morphing to "Marpi" and "Frajur" in my childhood. In my four Indian years I remember watching (with almost pornographic fascination) the afternoon perambulations of white-haired ladies in black dresses, under their parasols. "The widows' parade," my father called it, but later I learned they weren't widows at all. These were the Anglo-Indian wives whose British husbands had abandoned them for their ancient taint of Indian blood.

3. My father, the doctor, was a cautious man who made one impulsive decision in his life and that single gesture re-plotted the star-charts of everyone in the family. Forty years later, I have three sharp memories of India and the Nilingappa family compound that defined the world for my first four years.

I'm three years old. Little Dabu, the five-year-old son of Big Dabu, the mali, and I, are protecting banana flowers from a troop of monkeys. My mother had promised a side dish of *ballayephul palliya*, banana-flower curry, my favorite, for supper. Big Dabu had sharpened long, thin staves for us. Old Dabu (Big Dabu's father, Little Dabu's late grandfather), and Big Dabu and untold fathers and uncles had been Nilingappa-family malis ever since Mohan came to town. That night, my father slapped me at the dinner table, and I ran from my heroically protected banana-flower curry after announcing my desire to become a mali when I grew up.

Then I'm four years old. I remember the meagre tarmac of the old aerodrome and a prop-driven Indian Airlines plane that will take us to Bombay and the Air-India connection to London and the Trans-Canada flight to Montréal. Our bags – my father's old suitcases from his student days in Scotland, taller than I am – are lined up at the edge of the tarmac under a strip of awning. I remember the khaki-clad baggage-handler trying to chalk them, but I'm not allowing it. I keep wiping the chalk mark off; he says it's the law, a matter of security and identification, but I see it as an invasion of our property. He laughs as he leans down and begs me in our language, Kannada: *Baba, you must let me chalk the bags. It means you are safe to travel. You are going to America. You are the luckiest boy in the world.* This memory has lingered, I think, because I must have sensed my future. The Nilingappas, monarchs of Murphy Town, were being driven into permanent exile.

My father equated Canada with his simpler, carefree Edinburgh days. A place to wear his tweeds and enjoy a pint. What else could "Commonwealth" mean?

Forty years later, luck has landed me in a hotel room in Montréal, looking out on a city I can't begin to recognize. I tell myself I'm here for a funeral, except that the ceremony was three days ago, because no one knew how to find me. Or if they wanted.

The CNN crawl spews out its disjointed newsbits, ... *successful ship-to-ship transfer of more than one thousand luxury cruise passengers suffering acute intestinal distress ... police in Kansas City announce arrest of suspect in string of area murders* ... Terror alert: elevated ... *drug-doping investigation widening, major sports figures implicated* ... In weather news ... *first hurricane alert of the Atlantic season as Alexei gains strength* ...

4. Despite my father's professional status and comfortable income, he was only a second brother, and so his older brother had consigned our family to three rooms in the north wing. With my two older brothers we were a family of five, not counting our own cook and servants and their families. My younger uncle and his family had two rooms in the south wing. The rest, and it was considerable – a banquet hall, drawing rooms, salons, and tiled bathrooms with misting, brass boa constrictor water pipes and cobra showerheads capped with ruby eyes – was owned by my father's unemployed oldest brother and his retired, minor, Kannada-language film star wife. My father suffered constant second-son humiliation in a dysfunctional joint family. My mother survived, thanks to old servants and younger uncle's wife.

I was the youngest. My father said that "time to adjust" in the New World was on my side. I would be the great transmitter of Nilingappa family achievement to a new continent. Perhaps he only meant I would grow up without the trace of an Indian accent.

In that lone prediction, he was correct. We left behind grandparents, younger uncle and his wife, my cousins, Big and Little Dabu, and the usual retinue of cooks, servants, watchmen, drivers and their related and unrelated hangers-on. In India I had never, not for a minute of my life, been out of the sight of family or family retainers. Suddenly I was alone among strangers, and the streets, the city, the park, and every room in our first Canadian apartment was threatening.

When I was five years old, already fluent in English after six months of avid television watching – that cascade of transmission – I went from being Alok Nilingappa to being registered in an English-Protestant school as Alec. In Montréal forty years ago, a "Protestant" school usually meant Jewish-dominant, and "English-Catholic" meant immigrant Italian and Greek. My father associated Protestants with Edinburgh. French schools were available, but they were seriously Catholic, and he considered Roman Catholicism the religion of Goans and Anglo-Indians. What English-speaking immigrant to North America wants to turn out French-speaking children?

For my father, coming to Canada meant he could renew his fading memories of Scotland. How he loved the street names in English parts of the city! Clark, Craig, Drummond, Dufferin, MacEachran, Mackay, McGregor, Murray, Strathcona, Strathearn ... we always lived on Scottish-named streets.

My mother never adjusted. She fell into pious trances. She missed her retinue of servants. October snowflakes drove her indoors until blackfly season. She'd say the only thing worse than the joint-family – even a bad one – is life in a cold country without family or other friends or even the sight of other Indians. My brothers were New World successes. I became her anchor to India.

My brothers were old enough to speak and remember good

Kannada when they left. They were already resistant to the temptation of "corrupting influences." My oldest brother was one of
"Midnight's Children," born in 1947. For him, who was thirteen
and faintly moustached, there'd always be a trace of India in his
speech, and a heart divided. But money is docile, money follows
orders, money has no accent. A million by twenty-five seemed to
him a realizable goal, but it might be more. He studied the stock
pages of the morning *Gazette*. After Sir George Williams University,
he went to Ottawa and got an MBA. He was a natural networker. The
Liberals were in power, so he befriended well-placed Liberal staff-
ers. Tories, too. He was the avatar of Mohan Nilingappa. It didn't
bother him to be called "that smart little Indian guy from Montréal"
and other things behind his back. Eventually, he married Janelle, a
Québec girl; they spoke French at home. And in time he became
the seed money behind high-tech in Canada. Successes paid him
back ten- and twenty-fold. Later on, he opened the way to the out-
sourcing boom in Bangalore. He eventually founded a chair in
South Indian studies at Sir George.

And at fifty-nine, a week ago, he died.

My second brother was ten when we left. He too grew up in
Montréal without an accent, and less of a divided heart. He went to
McGill Law School, and – it being Québec – he practiced, eventually,
in French. He joined René Lévesque's Parti Québecois very early,
when independence for Québec seemed both natural and inevitable, and became a prominent "ethnic" component in an otherwise
homogenously Québecois party hierarchy.

As a four-year-old, the full burden of assimilation fell on me. I
had to learn the etiquette of survival in a bilingual, bicultural city,
when one is not, strictly speaking, part of the paradigm. Like the
Nilingappas of old, we lived comfortably but without intimacy
among the English. My school was English, and we were drilled in

French by Anglo teachers in the time-honoured manner of colonial administrators. The purpose of French instruction in the Protestant schools appeared to be inoculation against local usage. I never had my brothers' sturdy grounding in our Kannada language. To make the obvious pun, I had only Canada, and only half of that.

Before 1965 even got established, my father would pass his mandatory Canadian medical boards and set himself up in a practice. In India, he'd been a researcher with severely limited "clinic" hours; in Montréal he became a trusted family doctor. In those early years, when Indians were barely a presence in North America, he was seen as wise as well as competent, avuncular but authoritative. He could say to patients who'd traded in certainties all of their lives, "We of course can never be certain," and they would nod "of course not."

... Canada regains top prize ... UN releases annual Quality of Life results ... criteria based on personal income, environment, crime, housing availability and affordability, health care, life expectancy, infant mortality, political stability, educational standards and gender equality ... Rounding out top ten ... former #1 Norway falls to second, followed by 3. Australia, 4. Sweden, 5. Netherlands, 6. Belgium and 7. Denmark ... United States ranks 8; Japan 9 and Iceland rounds out top ten ...

In the Canada of my childhood, we might have smiled, or felt slightly embarrassed at such a ranking. What about the North, Newfoundland and the Maritimes? we might have asked. Stability? When our largest province wants to break away? When the courts are busting up public health? What cities did these UN guys visit, Vancouver and Toronto?

Now, three days back, I think the hordes of young people I see in the bistros and cafés would say, "*Regain?* When did we ever lose it?"

5. When I was seven years old, Expo '67 came to town. Suddenly we had a Métro system. The underground splendor of Place Ville-Marie was replicated in our neighborhood by Alexis Nihon Plaza and Westmount Place. Every stop on the Métro groomed its own gaudy, year-round-summertime, subterranean city. My oldest brother, Rajah, was twenty, then at Sir George. He talked himself into a job in the Indian pavilion at Expo. Early networking, this time with his fellow "workers", the privileged sons and daughters of high-ranking Indian politicians who'd somehow managed to place their children in such cushy circumstances. Middle brother, Suresh, was seventeen, the summer before he was to start out east, at Dalhousie. My mother decided I was deficient in Hindu knowledge, and so she began a project of epic proportions, bundling me up in bed with her and reading the *Mahabharata* in Kannada. My father went back to Bangalore for the summer, "to avoid the noise and crowds of Expo," he said.

The great Indian epic concerns an endless war between the armies of two brothers, the Pandavas and Kauravas. The battles are thrilling in their detail, even through the screen of my mother's telling in a language that will never be more than a second screen for me. "No hatred is greater than inside a family," she said. "Brothers will fight until no one is left, no home, no fields, no wife, no children." It was not much of a leap to read the epic as an intimate family melodrama, my father against his older brother. Older Uncle wanted to sell the estate; my father and younger uncle were against it, and willing to take their case to court.

Bangalore in 1967 was still the sleepy cantonment it had always been. But rumors of new money were filtering in, largely based on people like us, NRIS, non-resident Indians who wanted to return to India for retirement, but had grown accustomed to Western-style luxury after saving mountains of foreign exchange in the UK, Canada and us. Trusts were consolidating packages of farmland around Bangalore and floating huge building loans against inflated, overseas, hard-currency subscriptions. Not a brick had been laid, nor roads, nor services, and the land deeds were all in dispute and the "contractors" were crooks, but doctors and engineers who were too busy to visit muddy rice paddies were plunking down thousands of dollars for a precious lease, ten or fifteen years down the line. My oldest uncle had been approached. The grounds of Nilingappa Bhavan could easily accommodate a high-rise apartment block. The estate, of course, and the gardens, garages and tennis courts would all disappear. He stood to clear more rupees in one day than any Nilingappa had ever stashed under his mattress.

"The hell," my father said.

Uncle might have made (by my rough calculation) the equivalent of two hundred thousand 1967 dollars. In today's hi-tech Bangalore, even without tearing it down, the property might be worth five million. No one could have foreseen a time when Marpi Town would be a close-in suburb to a city of eight million hustlers, and home to five hundred overseas corporations. And thus was launched the suit and counter-suit, a war that would flare and subside for the next eighteen years as trial dates were set and delayed, bribes and counter-bribes paid; as judges retired and died, and lawyers moved onwards and upwards, and sometimes changed sides.

Father's message to my mother was: without total victory, without the expulsion of my brother and his fat whore of a wife, we're never going back. This cold, empty house, the snowploughs and snow-clearing – louder than a herd of panicked elephants, my mother would cry, hands over her ears – without Indian friends and with supermarkets full of unpalatable food under finger-numbing, impermeable plastic wrap, no banana flowers: this is your life. All your expertise negated; all your flaws exaggerated. We will fight him to the death, my father declared. This was a side of India, and even of my father, that seemed at odds with all I remembered and respected. At home, his rage was uncontainable; it terrified me. His plotting against Older Uncle was as elaborate and as fanciful as anything in the *Mahabharata*. Poisons, murder. Convenient accidents. And yet he was able to meet his patients day after day, the kindly, courtly, soft-spoken medical counselor.

6. In time, I too went to Sir George, although now they called it Concordia. It occupied an immense, worst-of-the-60s, cream-colored, fourteen-story office block between Mackay and Bishop, fronting on boul. de Maisonneuve. We were told, for what it's worth, that it was the largest educational building in the British Commonwealth. During the 70's and 80's, Concordia kept expanding, especially as old family businesses closed in the English-speaking west end. Apartment blocks were converted to offices of specialized programs. Across de Maisonneuve, another monster office block appeared, maybe the second largest in the Commonwealth.

Montréal of my college years was a different world from my brothers'. By the 80s, Indians were everywhere, though the demographic shift offered little social comfort to my mother. There were five Indian restaurants within two blocks of campus. Montréal was a French-speaking city now, signs were in French, and the Parti Québecois was in power. The English were selling out and moving west. The party outlawed the teaching of English to immigrant children. Had I arrived a dozen years later than I did, I would have become francophone, like the little Chinese, Indian, and Caribbean children I passed on the street and saw on the Métro; like the Italians and Greeks of the old English-Catholic schools. So far as any of us knew, Québec would be an independent country in a year or two. Despite the assurances of my middle brother, Suresh, my parents and I had no faith there'd be a place for us – non-French, non-English, now called "allophones" in the New Québec my brother and his comrades were building.

What to major in? My brothers had already split the world between Law and Commerce. Both were politicians, maybe even statesmen. If I'd wanted medicine I should have gone to McGill.

The one profession never mentioned and never permitted for an Indian son is anything remotely approaching the arts. "Every son of India who writes or acts or paints is a family tragedy," my father used to say, and my mother probably agreed. But I was drawn to the arts, and the most dangerous art, as I plodded through a pre-architectural degree.

My father also promised to do his duty to me and find a bride. I took a good picture, and he was rich and "situated" so he was confident of a successful match. He wanted to find a good Bangalorean girl. My brothers were too independent. They dated Canadian girls, but I was a good boy, I didn't date.

Meanwhile, property values were plunging and my father decided our future would have to have a Toronto address. The English-speakers who left Québec for the rest of Canada and those allophones who sided with them were called Rhodesians. Call me what you will; it was my one honourable chance to get away, and I knew if I didn't grab it, my life was over. I called myself British Columbian. I applied to the graduate school of architecture at UBC.

Theatre Arts accepted me.

You've guessed, haven't you? Who I am, and what I became? Especially if I say the blessing and the curse of my post-adolescent life is that I grew into extraordinary handsomeness. Too handsome to be trusted, too handsome to be anything but a replica of handsomeness, like a credit card version of wealth. I became an actor. Does the caterpillar know he will some day fly? (I always did.)

7. This morning I called my (late? former? ex-? *feu?*) *belle-sœur*, sister-in-law, Janelle Nilingappa-Desrosiers, attempting to express my sympathies. I was a week late for my brother's *shradh*, the cremation and ceremonial death-service. Excusably inexcusable, I felt, since I live in Los Angeles and news from Canada barely penetrates. I learned of my brother's death only when an old Montréal friend called, surprised I was still at home and not in Canada. Janelle and my brother had been married nearly ten years, though I've never met her.

Janelle, c'est Alok, ton beau-frère, d'la Californie. (I waited. Nothing.) *Personne ne m'a informé.* (No one told me.) *Je viens d'arriver à Montréal.* (I just got in.) *Je suis desolé. Je regrette profondement ce qu'il c'est passé, et j'éprouve de la sympathie pour toute la famille.*

Quel beau-frère? (What brother-in-law?) *Je n'y ai pas.* (I don't have one.) *Vous avez le mauvais numéro. Décrochez. Ne m'inquietez plus.* (Wrong number. Hang up. Don't bother me anymore.)

Janelle, s'il te plaîs, je peux m'expliquer ... puis-je te visiter?

Quel type de sicko es-tu? Vas t'en foûtre.

Janelle, ton mari, Rajah, avait deux frères. Nous étions trois. Rajah, Suresh et Alok. Rajah était l'aîné. Moi, je suis le cadet.

Vas t'enculer, tu, tu ... sac de merde. (Go fuck yourself, shit-sack). *Je n'ai plus mon mari. Je suis veuve.* (I don't have my husband anymore. I'm a widow.)

I can tell you're a little stressed, Janelle. Grieving. Maybe this isn't a good time.

As I fumbled through my profound sympathies, I realized she wasn't just stressed – she didn't have *la moindre idée* of who I was. Rajah and I were the last Nilingappas, but my brother had excluded me from the family, cast me into some kind of Indian family *salon de refusés*. For what, exactly, I don't know, but it isn't hard to guess. I wasn't invited to their marriage ceremony, either.

8. After the call I went walking from my hotel, looking for something solid, something recognizable in the city that formed me. The only thing I could think of was my alma mater, squat, ugly old Concordia. If I couldn't send my sympathies directly to Janelle, at least I could leave them off at the Nilingappa Centre for South Indian Studies. The walk between Concordia and the Queen Elizabeth Hotel, along Dorchester or de Maisonneuve, past Phillips Square, is something I've done a hundred times. Of course, the street names have changed and the low, undistinguished buildings have been razed and replaced with new towers, each of them with food courts and underground mini-malls and access to Métro stops I didn't know existed, and new hotels with lines of Euro-trash tourist buses outside and liveried doormen to unload their dozens of bags.

It occurred to me that if none of us had ever moved, if my father had patched things up with his brother and we'd stayed in Bangalore, or if I'd stayed in Montréal, we'd all be richer and more at peace with the world. Blips in the market come and go; one mustn't uproot oneself in panicked reaction. Montréal is a beautiful, sophisticated city and Canada has the highest Quality of Life in the world. My brother Suresh was right, it's better that everyone speaks French ("the Frencher the better," he used to say, "it's just like India. Every state gets its own language," and he was too big for our outraged father to slap him.) If I had stayed, I'd be one of the Montréalais I hear in the hotel bar, or on the streets, whose mastery of English is indistinguishable from his French.

And now that cascade of transmission – regret, confusion – settles in. I remember my theatre classes, and then my roles, all my reviews, the regret that I was never able to share them with my parents who patiently waited for their architect-butterfly to stagger from his cocoon. Vancouver theatre to West Coast theatre, to television, to movies, to a final home in California; it looks so easy, so inevitable. I changed my name and I used to hide news of my appearances, hoping that minor celebrity profiles would not be reprinted east of Edmonton.

I remember the great news from my father: his older brother had fallen ill, and wanted to settle. And so he and my mother and the family lawyer – our brilliant Suresh – were off to Bangalore to seal the deal. My parents were sixty years old and ready for retirement, not in a sterile new condo with all the conveniences, but in the dowdy/stately luxury of Nilingappa Bhavan. Toronto was nice, they said, but rather anti-Indian in a crude, working-class, British sort of way – although the absence of French was compensation. They'd given twenty-one years to Canada and left the country with three productive citizens. What more can be asked?

"How handsome you've become!" my mother exclaimed, at our going-away (or going-back) dinner. My father took new pictures and joked, "When I come back, I'll bring your bride with us." "Are you sure you don't want to come?" my mother begged. "It's never too late," my father said. I told him I had to get back to classes. A practicum, I remember saying. Something we were doing down in Seattle. Suresh, I could tell, wasn't fooled.

It was a cool June evening and my father was wearing his usual Scottish woolens. They'd all be off on Air-India next morning, big parting ceremony at the airport. Next morning, I watched them leave. They never arrived, and they never came back.

And by the time I relive the horror of losing my family, except for Rajah, I'm lost. I keep walking west, then north on Mountain, and west again on René Lévesque past Crescent, to Bishop, then up to de Maisonneuve – and the two giant Concordia University buildings are gone. The biggest educational building in the Commonwealth *n'est plus*. I know the area, I know I'm in the right place, but the forces of transformation have taken it away, and if I don't know where Concordia is, what in this world do I know at all? If Dorchester is now René-Lévesque, what is de Maisonneuve without my university? I'm standing at the ground zero of my life as a Canadian and as an immigrant, as a boy-turned-man trying to imitate the ways of manhood, and the ground has disappeared.

9. I remember reading a John Cheever story in a Concordia English class, about the demented man who thinks he can swim across his suburban county by swimming a lap in all its backyard pools. "An allegory," the professor said, of life itself, starting young, frisky, revisiting the women he's known, taking a drink, crashing parties, then the pools grow scummy and untended and the women scorn him and he hears rumors of his bad behavior, some shameful rumors, and the day grows cooler, and the houses are boarded up and still he pursues his crazy dream until he's an old man standing on the side of a road. Maybe I forget part of it. I saw the movie, with Burt Lancaster, and something was lost. In today's Montréal it might be possible to link the city underground. You could have a drink in maybe eighty or a hundred bars along a single Métro line.

Father's younger brother, who never left his two rooms in Bangalore, inherited the entire estate. He's worth ten million, I hear.

I'm sitting at a "sidewalk" table of a coffee shop in the CN station underneath the Queen Elizabeth Hotel, looking up at the steady green lights of the departures board. Times and destinations bounce off the board like the CNN crawl: suburban trains, then the VIA Rails to New York, Toronto, Ottawa and Halifax.

I am now, truly, alone in the world, a middle-aged orphan.

When I was little, I used to come down here – when it was a vast, concrete hangar devoid of any décor, before the bistros, boulanges and charcuteries – to see my brothers off to their colleges, then, later, when I ventured down to New York or Toronto, allegedly for architectural research.

A young woman approaches. Very short skirt, fuzzy sweater, long, lank blondish hair, holding a legal pad to her breast. "*Vous permettez?*" she asks, and I pull out the second chair to accommodate her.

"*Français/anglais?*" she asks, and I commit the Rhodesian sin, at least the sin of twenty years ago, saying, "My English is much better."

She holds out her hand. "Marie-Louise Tremblay."

"Al Neeling," I say.

"May I ask a personal question, Mr. Neeling? You have a very strong presence. Have you ever acted?"

I nod. "I have my SAG card."

"Wow, that's impressive. I'm casting for Jean-Luc Carrier." It's a name I'm familiar with. French-language, foreign films, art-house. Ten screens nationwide, max.

"He's casting for his first English-language film. He has Hollywood backing. It will be shot here. He's sitting just over there." I follow her eyes, and a smallish man, gray hair, tight beard, leather jacket, nods. A very familiar look. "M'sieur Carrier said to me: that man is perfect. You can't take your eyes off him." She giggles, and draws a little closer. "He said, 'I'll rewrite the script to get him in. Beg him to audition.' So I'm doing the begging for him." Marie-Louise, I notice, has absolutely no accent.

"Please don't beg on my account, Marie-Louise. And please convey my respects to m'sieur Carrier. I'm very flattered, really. But I'm here for family business and I have to get back to L.A. *tout de suite,*" which is a lie. "Rehearsals, you understand."

She looks crushed, as though I'd reached across and slapped her. Her eyes say, *perhaps you didn't hear me: I said Jean-Luc Carrier.* She fishes around for a business card. "In case you change your mind, Mister Neeling?"

I tell her I might very well.

"You're very beautiful," she says. "More than handsome."

I tell her I wish I could stay. But I can't go back; obliteration is gaining on me. It's this journey I've started, it's the old women and their parasols, the meagre tarmac and the banana flowers, all the Nilingappa dead and those unmailed clippings in my drawer. I don't know where it will end, I just pick up identities, play them with all the passion I'm capable of, and then I throw them away. Tomorrow I'll be back in L.A.

A CONNIE DA CUNHA BOOK

CONNIE'S FATHER had been a teacher, and general promoter of the Portuguese language and Luso-Indian culture in the seaside Goan village of Caranzalem. Portuguese, he believed, had protected Goa from the tragic fate of India. Their cottage functioned as a community library of French, Spanish and Portuguese texts and their back lawn, between monsoons, had been outfitted with a modest stage and commercial lighting. Connie and her brothers used to sit at their father's feet in the tropical, sea-breezy evenings, citronella candles sputtering, while he read passages from French and Spanish classics and asked his children to act out the same scenes in Portuguese. Despite her profession and current residence – book editor in New York – Portuguese remained her comfort language; it provides the music she plays, the wisdom she quotes and the pork and fish vindaloos that she cooks for private celebrations.

Back in her London years she'd known exiled Indonesian writers, some of whom had been imprisoned and tortured by the colonial regime, who still – in the evening, over tumblers of Scotch – reverted to Dutch among themselves. It is a tight, mysterious fraternity, those who grew up with unconsummated love or complicated hate for their colonial masters. Understanding the dynamic had made her the person, and the editor she was.

When the Indian Army invaded the Portuguese colony in 1962, her father's life unraveled. Anyone closely identified with the Portuguese regime, those with Portuguese passports, was encouraged to leave. Many of her relatives did just that; even her father explored emigration to Macao. Her favorite uncle, Narciso Salgado, left his large congregation in Panjim and secured a position as an assistant priest in an Azorean diocese in Massachusetts.

For Connie, then six years of age and named Conceição, the loss of language and country was overcome in less than a month. She was shifted from second standard in a Portuguese school run by nuns to First Standard English and Hindi, taught by a retired ICS officer named Govind Sharma, an exacting schoolmaster with Oxford experience. "I'm not your enemy," he said on that first day, in a language she'd rarely heard but oddly, half-understood. "We're not identical, but we are part of each other. I will say that in Hindi, your new language, and you will understand me. *Hum aapney dushman nahii hai, lekin aapkey saha yogi hai.* I will not tolerate a single word of the former language, either in the classroom or on school property." Two months later, she read her first English book, *We Are Six*.

Within a few weeks, Master Sharma promoted her to third standard. Her father, removed from teaching, opened a small Portuguese bar and restaurant, and eventually the family prospered. But a teacher's hours are not a bartender's, and the evening readings and staged events ended. One of her brothers won a scholarship to Portugal, she and another brother to Britain. Her baby brother, Ferdy, who'd been born after the Indian invasion, never left Goa. He was happily Indian and ran a construction company, putting up sea-facing condos for Europeans, Israelis, and rich Bombayites.

Connie knew she would be an editor, and she knew it at the age of eight or nine. There were no book editors in Goa. She simply knew that she had a calling. Whenever she started reading a book, she did not think of teaching it, writing it, or publishing it. Before she learned the word "editor" she sensed there must be an invisible hand guiding it, shaping it, giving it birth. It was her uncle Narciso, on his first visit home, who remarked, "Eight years old, and she's already correcting my English! She'll be an editor, for sure." He would reward her by allowing a drag on his cigarette.

Connie was outside Café Alsacien finishing a second smoke when Cynthia Freeman, a debut author using the name *Ramonah!* pulled up in a chauffeur-driven Town Car. She was dressed in her self-proclaimed *haute dyke* battle gear: blacker-than-black, chewed-end hair, fishnet stockings, six-inch heels, spiky silver accessories and a glistening, bright red vinyl jacket with a matching miniskirt that crinkled as she walked. She looked and sounded like a piece of hard candy wrapped in red cellophane. Her nails were lacquered an arterial crimson, her lips a venous reddish-brown. Connie had never felt so dull and squat.

Before her *Ramonah!* incarnation – the exclamation point suggested by a chance-sighting of a *Utah!* license plate – Cynthia Freeman had been a Bronx-based paralegal with dreams of Africa. She'd gone to Kenya and Tanzania on a photo safari and fallen in love with a Masai herdswoman named Mbala. Mbala had pressed Cynthia's face to her bare breasts and through those mighty gourds intoned ancient tribal wisdom. She also proved to be a canny publicist and wardrobe consultant. She stretched Cynthia's neck with five steel rings – magically stoking her sluggish metabolism – and told her that she would soon be beautiful, rich and powerful by following a few simple rules. First: overcoming doubt and fear. Antelopes fear; lions do not. Second: getting in touch with her inner lion. Mbala gave her a name: "Dykalah", and from that moment on, Cynthia Freeman began to roar. She returned to The Bronx and transcribed all nine hundred of Mbala's "breast words" into a five-page proposal for which, after a spirited bidding war, she pocketed a million and a half dollars, movie rights and twenty translations to follow. A million and a half for a five-page, cockamamie proposal? Those were the days.

Connie da Cunha was assigned the editing. For *Ramonah!* the serious part of writing involved accumulating a new wardrobe, hiring publicists, make-up consultants and a personal trainer. Editing meant "fleshing out" the remaining seventy thousand words around the chapter titles. *Ramonah!*'s prowling inner lion lent viable terror to the concept of "fleshing out." To Connie, it meant someone, probably her, having to induce a book to justify the advance.

Connie and *Ramonah!* fought through months of *Mbala would never say that! Show my readers how my awakening Dykalah-self frightened me in the beginning! Why was I chosen? I was like Mary at the Annunciation! Show my doubts, my vulnerability, despite my obvious beauty, talent, strength and confidence. Show me in the cage with Dykalah! Show how I fed my old Cynthia body and soul to her. Show the old Cynthia disappearing bite by bite and the new Ramonah! growing more and more human. Share my journey! Can't you just do that?* This, after all, is what editors were put on earth, or at least in Manhattan, to do.

Despite *Ramonah!*'s outrageousness, the narrow channel between provocative and irritating she navigated, the self-dramatization, the mismatch between her talent and its reward, Connie found herself halfway in thrall. At times, she thought of *Ramonah!* embodying some lost part of herself, her confident, sassy past. Though she could never assert it, and *Ramonah!* would shriek at the suggestion, they were sisters. There really was, out there in the savannahs of east Africa, a Mbala. Cynthia had taken her picture with her cellphone. She resembled Smokin' Joe Frazier, the one-time boxer, but with commanding breasts. As *Ramonah!* explained it, "Mbala feels that inside us there are mouse genes and a reptile brain, so why not an inner lion?"

Pretty sophisticated thinking, Connie had thought.

"Loved it!" *Ramonah!* said, squeezing Connie's hand and landing a sticky kiss in the centre of her cheek. (What part of writing does she love, Connie wondered – the book jacket? The full, back-cover color photo? The combined book-and-motivational-speaker's tour?) At least now, finally, there was a physical book and soon there would be reviews, a tour and interviews. Heads turned as the maitre d' led them to a corner table. "My goodness," the author dropped her voice to a leonine rumble, "the Lesbians are out in force today." Café Alsacien was a safe house for midtown's professional ladies: the agents, editors, lawyers and performers. No cheap-ticket matinee theatergoers, no mall-escapees, no tourists, very few men. A table of midtown ladies stared obliquely, then picked up their drinks in unison. "I think they're staring at *you*, dear," Connie tried, thinking, *I know I would*. "Of course they are," *Ramonah!* agreed. "And they're so deliciously jealous."

Poppycock, she wanted to say. Then, modestly, "They don't have the slightest idea of who I am."

"Of course not. But they know who you're with." She raked the hand of her editor, drawing blood. Her inner lion was on the prowl. "I didn't think another dyke would object," she said.

"Another what?"

"Oh, get with it, Connie. Every halfway sensible woman's a Lesbian, but only a few can be dykes. Mbala's fourth rule. First, be a dyke and you can aspire to becoming a Queer."

Mbala was a continuous surprise, Connie thought. "I'd forgotten," she said.

Ramonah! had been working with Connie for over a year without ever asking "da Cunha? What kind of name is that?" She never asked about the origins of Connie's slightly British accent. She never asked if there was a husband, children, or a partner of any sort. One day at Pão, in TriBeCa, Connie had said to the waiter, "*O pão é rei da mesa*" – bread is king of the table – and the waiter had responded, and she had said something further, and *Ramonah!* had whacked her dinner knife sharply on the table. *You will never upstage me in public again! I know they must have stuffed you full of languages wherever you came from, but I won't have you regurgitating them over lunch! Only if you knew Kiswahili might you be helpful. Otherwise, kindly hold your tongue.* The lone exception to the no-foreign-language rule was brief, semi-private messages exchanged between Connie and taxi drivers, in Hindi. *Ramonah!* assumed that one trip to Africa and one afternoon's quasi-intimate connection with an African woman marked her as more daring and more cosmopolitan than any other Manhattan woman, let alone a foreign-born editor. An editor's job was to offer suggestions in such a way that they could be immediately rejected but ultimately incorporated.

In her *Ramonah!* persona, Cynthia referred to every woman, except for beneath-contempt Lesbians, as dykes. She called their waitperson "a sturdy serving dyke," and held her hand as she laid out an elaborate order. "And where do you work out, dear? I can get you into my gym anytime. My PT does Sandra Bernhard. The salad's okay, but tell the chef no lemon in the dressing. I'm sure the little faggot has an interesting fruity vinegar. No flour and definitely no cornstarch in any of the sauces. I have no problem with the fish – but why does he? Don't even try to serve me those ghastly preboiled potatoes. If I have to go back to the kitchen, it won't be pretty."

Ramonah! inserted a cigarette in her lips but didn't light it. Half the clientele flinched in their seats, ready to pounce. She took out a flashy silver lighter. The ladies at the nearest table began flapping their arms, "No smoking!" She set the unlit cigarette, imprinted in lipstick, balanced on the edge of the bread plate. She lifted it and studied the lipstick traces. "So-o-o Joan Crawford, don't you think?" Lipstick on a cigarette; Connie could respond to that, although she'd never worn make-up. "When I started going to movies that was the sexiest thing I ever saw."

"We could go out for a smoke," Connie suggested. Joan Crawford was not part of her childhood.

Hours later, back home, Connie still bore the scabs. Oh, she's a cat.

Breastwords is not what the industry will recognize as a Connie da Cunha book, although Teddy Jenkins, the publisher, had insisted that only she could put it across. Connie's books were usually set among shadowy immigrant communities in London or New York. They featured potent memories of an ancestral homeland, twisted loyalties, religious and sexual and political schisms. Connie had introduced a London audience to the south Asians and Nigerians and Jamaicans in their midst, then Teddy had lured her to New York to do the same in America. Over the years, she'd edited six Nobel Prize winners. *Ramonah!* and her Masai were just another shadow society.

Connie didn't think of herself as a New Yorker, but she'd been there twelve years and she couldn't go back to London or Bombay or anywhere. She was effectively trapped in New York. No airline permitted smoking, and she could not endure an hour without a smoke.

Her above-tree-level view of Central Park from the east-facing living room and study was a sign of having arrived in the world of high-powered New York editing. Also the fact that there was an imprint, *A Connie da Cunha Book,* occupying one featured shelf in the living room. Apart from a half-wall of a mirror surrounded by plaques, awards and framed photographs, not another inch of wall space was given over to anything but books, the newer ones stashed horizontally on top of earlier acquisitions, like a second wave of destruction from a mass kill-off. Corners of the spare bedrooms and library had not been dusted in at least five years. She and Sam had no interesting furniture or decor. It's as though she'd been wooed from her London job with the promise of pay and power and grand professional advancement, but had failed to negotiate an entertainment, decorative or wardrobe budget. Or, that she'd never intended to stay. She lived like a renter, with rented furniture.

She looked up from a Jamaican novel she was editing and stared at herself in the ornate mirror over her desk and declared, I am over fifty years old and have lived these past fifteen years with a woman. When we sleep, I hold my hand over her breast and the dark outline of her downiness. Unlike the gazelle-slim, Lycra-clad, spiky-haired *Ramonah!* Connie was overweight, smoked too much and cared too little for her appearance. "Sam," she called, "has the time come to think of us as dykes? To come out, as it were?"

"You've been with your Lion Queen again," came the response from the bathroom. "Shall I bring out the Band-Aids?"

"Or would a coming-out party be redundant?"

"I for one have never been with a man," said Sam. "You are the most exciting and beautiful woman I've ever seen. Everyone must assume we're Lesbians at least, so who cares?"

She thought, I said dyke, not Lesbian.

Unlike Sam and maybe *Ramonah!* Connie had been with many men. When she'd arrived as a 22-year-old fresh from Bombay, London had paid *Ramonah!*-like attention. Conceição da Cunha, Connie, dark beauty, brilliant and acerbic, seen in all the right clubs, mentoring an emergent community that would soon take over. She'd been involved with a string of unsuitable men, many of them married and looking for an exotic night out. But no proper man had come along. Sam had. And when Teddy's offer came, Sam was part of the package. Probably she was right. Their relationship was known, and rather ordinary for the times, and place.

"Anyway," said Sam, "don't dykes use contraptions? Strap-on things? I could go online if you want to try."

I just want to cuddle, thought Connie.

Back in her wild London days, there'd been a newspaper caption to one of her glamour shots, stepping from a limo. *Gentlemen of the Evening: Sophia Loren may be a reach, but there's a certain young lady nearly as shapely, who, we hear, always says yes.*

Until the afternoon at Café Alsacien, prompted by the histrionic outpourings of *Ramonah!* she'd never thought of herself as belonging to any particular category. Her identity was couched in a series of nots: not a citizen, not married, not old, not young. She felt herself a big-city person, equally at ease in London, Bombay, or New York. "Unmarried" was just another line on the tax return, revisable should she encounter a literate, tolerant, adventurous and accommodating male, or if American marriage laws changed and Sam made an honest woman of her. She did not long for a man, or a woman, nor feel her life in any way unfulfilled. She couldn't muster a gut-wrenching aversion to men, or the deep sexual loathing of *Ramonah!* When *Ramonah!* spoke of ridding the world of hegemonic priapistic rapists, a world cleansed of phallic dominance, Connie merely smiled and assigned such declarations to Mbala.

It was Connie who'd actually, truly, killed a man.

It was back in Goa. She'd just completed college in Bombay, and had a scholarship to England. She'd taken a month off to say goodbye to baby-brother Ferdy and her parents. It was a warm, misty day. She'd decided to walk along the beach highway until she found some sort of kiosk selling *The Times of India* and cigarettes. The kiosk was on the far side of the highway and she stepped into her lane, which was bare except for a boy on a bicycle several meters away. When she got to the middle, she realized her mistake: four years in Bombay, navigating through unbroken walls of traffic, had induced an expectation of order. People crossed streets in Bombay all the time. They got to the middle, stood a moment behind a rough lane-divider, a concrete pylon perhaps, or a narrow, raised median, then dashed for the far side at the merest hint of a let-up in traffic. But on the beach highway in Goa, there were no dividers. Goa traffic used the entire road in each direction, flinching before oncoming traffic only at the last minute. Now she was some suicidally stupid creature, standing in the middle of a highway, who had forgotten how to cross a road. One driver, shouting at her and waving his arm, slapped on his brakes, honking and screeching and cursing, and another car skidded out of its lane and struck the young man on his bicycle.

"Run, lady, run!" the witnesses cried, and she did, knowing the summary fate of any driver, or perhaps any pedestrian, for having caused a fatal road accident. Even as she ran, she was thinking: *I am not the author. I am just the editor.* And thirty years later, at night, she could hear the hollow, watermelon crunch of a tire crushing the biker's skull. The boy's name was Leandro Hernandes, sixteen years old, a name that would hang around her neck the rest of her life.

Life is a riotous fusion. She'd always suspected that important decisions are backed into, slid into, and on occasion even stumbled over. No brave proclamation. No Mbala-style manifesto. One minute, I'm crossing the road for a pack of cigarettes, and a boy is killed. One day I'm the toast of London, the new "it" girl, and twenty-five years later I'm a pudgy Manhattan Lezzie.

She was a New Yorker because twelve years ago she'd received an invitation from Teddy Jenkins to leave London and become a senior editor at America's most prestigious publisher. And when she'd boarded the plane at Heathrow, strapped in business class for the seven-hour flight, and she'd inserted her customary take-off cigarette, flight attendants surrounded her, flapping their arms, "No smoking! No smoking!"

"I'll go into the bathroom, then," she'd said. They said that would not be acceptable. But that meant she would have to fly all the way to New York without a cigarette, and she hadn't been deprived of a smoke for more than an hour anytime in the past twenty years. Every cigarette carried with it the residual pleasures of warmth and love, the soft, tropical dark and the mysterious beauty of languages.

She'd made a spectacle of herself, running up and down the aisles, pleading and crying, then threatening, offering money for a suspension of the rules, until the captain was called and the FBI alerted on the landing end. She was warned that she'd be placed on a no-fly list and she'd never be allowed to fly on any airliner again. She was suddenly a prisoner, exile and criminal. After the bombings in New York, she was automatically transferred to a terrorist list.

Her parents were dead, her brothers well-settled. She had no one to answer to, no reasons for apology or subterfuge. All she had was a shelf of books she'd edited, a wall of professional plaques, photos and awards, a tobacco addiction, and Sam. All she asked was, let me smoke, let me drink, let me shuffle, not jog, from Central Park West and Seventy-Sixth to my office on East Fifty-Second.

Life's a spectrum, and I've never moved more than a step or two from the middle.

Another day, outside the brass-framed doors, smoking, Teddy mentioned there were rumours around. That's what the book business is – the packaging and repackaging of rumours. Only these might be true.

She and Teddy Jenkins met for their breaks ten minutes at the top of every hour. The fresh air, hot or cold, relief from fine print, was welcome. Connie was still waiting for the quintessential modern romantic comedy based on cigarette-breaks: young people standing in the cold, appealingly ashamed of their addiction, a little brazen about their risk-taking. But people who smoke can't be funny or loveable or even admirable in modern America.

Teddy held his cigarette high, right elbow propped on left wrist, *so Joan Crawford*, Connie thought. He tapped the ash over his right shoulder. She cupped hers, a furtive habit begun in her Catholic girls' college in Bombay. She smoked like the shadowy limo drivers lining the block: cigarettes cupped, polishing a fender, waiting for their clients.

"There's a buzz building. Your African Queen book."

"A-wim-a-way, a-wim-a-way," Connie hummed.

"Ah, the jungle, the mighty jungle. Publicity's all over me. They don't know what to make of this *Ramonah!* thing. How do we present it? Memoir? Travel? Race? God help us, Gay Lit?"

"It's a Third World narrative," said Connie. "It's my autobiography with African names."

"Ah, the madly popular Third World autobiography. Did I tell you about the bidding war for Kofi Annan's memoirs? No?"

It was Connie's belief that even a drop of immigrant blood from any of the world's inhospitable corners held more storylines than any famous American book ever written. The exceptions proved it: *Moby-Dick*, *Absalom, Absalom! Beloved, Invisible Man*.

"When we're finished with your African Queen, we'll start work on Jimmie. That will be a blockbuster."

Teddy Jenkins and Jimmie Dos Santos were a Page Six couple. *Ramonah!* called Teddy a male-dyke, a great compliment, but Jimmie Dos Santos was Queer. Jimmie had crossed to Manhattan from Queens, a beautiful boy with chorus-boy ambitions, a high school dropout shunned by his Brazilian immigrant family. He'd started out in Manhattan as a countertenor in the Gay Men's Chorus. He wrote and performed "I Sing of Myself," one of the greatest romantic duets ever, a duet of one, his rich baritone seducing his aerial alto. He danced and sang and acted and wrote and directed and produced his way to stardom and homes on three continents. And he owed it all to sex ("Oh, for God's sake, Conceição, wipe that disapproving Catholic schoolgirl frown right off your face!"), to something Greek or maybe Renaissance in its fluted perfection. Exuberant but contained, flared but folded, more Cellini than Michelangelo. An early critic had called him a Fabergé Egg, "decorative, but hollow," and lived to regret it.

Today Teddy said, "I often wonder what might happen if I lay my head on your naked bosom. What would I hear?"

In her pert London years, she might have said *these boobs are made for gawking*. "We could see. I'm free at three."

"Connie, you know I love it when you channel Dr. Seuss. But I've got meetings at three and four."

"My bosom waits for no man."

"So I hear," said Teddy.

"You said two rumours?" she asked.

He dropped his voice to executive depth. "This one is less fun. It seems we're going to be bought out by a Liechtenstein-based consortium."

"I didn't know Liechtenstein did publishing."

"Our new mystery-owners made their fortune in surgical glues and Spanish condominia."

"Glues, plural? Like the Glues Brothers? The things one learns. And condominia, that's good."

"I have enough self-respect not say consortium and condominium in the same sentence. Glues Brothers: a joke, like the old days. It would be funny if it weren't so terribly, terribly sad. Connie," he added, and his voice dropped with funereal gravity, "the party's over. The dream, the privilege, bringing you over from London, the lunches, the great books we managed to publish while having so much fun, even the silliness ... it's gone. These things never happen overnight. I think we're operating as usual until ... maybe Monday. Jimmie and I are legends, so we can retire to one of his legendary palaces. I'm thinking of Vieques. You and Sam can stay there as long as you like, and when you get bored, he's got ten more places, all of them staffed and furnished. I wish I could have looked after you better. I thought literature was forever. What a fool I was."

Connie thought: *Breastwords* will be our last major success. Maybe we deserve to die.

Maybe the time has come to be the author, not the editor of my life.

It's amazing how rapidly things can move in modern America. One day you're a senior editor of a publishing house with a hundred and fifty year history of bringing out nearly every significant book in the American canon, and nearly every European Nobel Prize winner, and the new Asians and Africans and Caribbeans, and the next day moving vans have lined the block, your locks are changed, and you and Teddy Jenkins can be found (on the evening news) throwing yourselves over stuffed boxes and lying down in front of handcarts loaded with desks and books and pictures and filing cabinets. "Doesn't anyone care?" you scream. To a contingent of burly, blank-faced office-cleaners, Teddy Jenkins – lately the darling of Page Six – cries out, "Sinclair Lewis is in that box! He won the Nobel!"

By nightfall, the files and correspondences had been shifted to a landfill in New Jersey. An injunction to halt the "Slaughter on Fifty-

Second Street" arrived too late. The Glues Brothers had not investi-gated the possibility of museums and universities bidding on a collection, or the absurdity of private citizens paying serious money for scraps of ancient paper. They'd seen a mid-town tower, a crumbling dollar, the soaring Euro and a teetering major tenant. A steal, just waiting to be brought up to code and converted to mixed use.

The Glues Brothers – whose names and country of origin re-mained matters of conjecture – allowed her six months' severance and rent on her apartment. After that, she and Sam, their furniture, books, plaques and awards, would be out on the sidewalk, and a few months later, the old rent-controlled apartment, the last in the building, would be remodeled, condo-ized and put on the market for three point five million. She of course would be allowed to bid.

Scanning the Internet for specialized sites, Sam came across an ad for "LavendAir", a welcoming carrier for "Smokin' Hot Dykes". It was the world's first all-Queer airline, for "smokers and gropers", and in-air weddings. As Jimmie Dos Santos said, "get eighty of your closest friends together and charter it for anywhere. Eighty dykes dropping in on Goa? No problem." She and Sam were married somewhere in legal airspace over Canada.

They were headed to Goa to stay in a house in a "colony" of forty modern sea-facing cottages built by her little brother, Ferdy. Where else could she go, an unemployed fifty-something with a dwindling retirement account? She hadn't seen Ferdy in over thirty years, since the week she'd spent in Goa before going off to Britain. The week she'd failed to cross the road. Leandro Hernandes.

"I'll be bringing my wife," she'd said on the phone.

"Great," said Ferdy, "we get lots of Europeans."

Indeed they did, half of the men of Germany, from what she could see from the verandah where she'd set up her computer, a drink, and cigarettes. They were out there on the pathways, walrus-like, in flesh-coloured thongs.

And so, in a modern, sea-facing house with all the amenities, on land that Ferdy had assembled atop the very soil of their childhood home, she began her Third World memoir, her chance to show that a single drop of blood from the world's most distant corner contains more narrative, more character, more life, than the major streets of the major cities. Yes, I have loved men and women and I am responsible for a death, I have seen the collapse of empire and the rise of the new, and I know all the famous people in my profession, and the stories surrounding them.

But I have done it all as an observer.

Two months into her writing, in a chapter called *We Are Six*, remembering the first English-language book she'd read, and how she'd connected it to the six members of her family, as she dealt with the Indian takeover of Goa, her father's loss of purpose, and learning English in classes led by Govind Sharma, she realized she was just another colonial *olla podrida* of jumbled languages, passports and lovers. The columns she'd filled in – editor, cosmopolitan – to mix her metaphors, are the common baggage, the DNA, of the Third World Immigrant. Being an editor saved her from having to create an identity of her own. Oh, for the surgical certainty of *Ramonah!* She'd spent a life straightening other people's creations, pinching the language here and there. What could be her ending? The lives of people like her seemed the endless middle of an unticketed journey. The pack of cigarettes stayed unopened next to her computer.

She had her own Mbala, who'd been with her all these years, alive in her memories and in her heart. *We are not identical, but we are part of each other.* She had never forgotten.

WAITING FOR ROMESH

THESE ARE THE RANDOM THOUGHTS, over a late afternoon and early evening, of a balding man waiting for his friend. What is the evolutionary advantage of thinning hair? Could it be that balding apes sensed heat and rain before their hirsute brethren, knowing to seek shelter, thus having more playtime to pass on their genes?

According to theory, one monkey out of an infinite number working on an infinite bank of typewriters will create a flawless draft of *King Lear*. It puts a human face on the notion of "infinity." Two or three might come close, misspelling a word or deleting a comma, which seems somehow even more miraculous, more human, and tragic. It signals a failed intent. Perfection seems just a more refined form of accident.

Higher altitudes are cooler because fewer molecules are available for collision, thus releasing energy. Given infinite time, every molecule in a confined space – even if the molecules represent the world's population and the confined space is earth itself – makes contact with every other.

All roads lead to Rome. It is said that if one sits long enough at a café on the Via Veneto, everyone he has ever known will eventually pass by. This has not proven to be the case, however, for Cyrus Chutneywala of Baroda, Gujarat, seated this afternoon at The Factory Tavern in Andy Warhol Square, Pittsburgh. Cyrus, called Chutt by his Indian friends and Chuck by his colleagues at the Mellon Bank, has been waiting through a long afternoon, dinnertime and now early evening for his Wharton batch-mate, Romesh Kumar.

"I hope you weren't offended," the waitress said half an hour earlier, when she set his third narrow flute of beer – this one on the house – in front of him. She is tall and thin, wearing black jeans and a slack, black cutaway T-shirt. He searches for the proper word: singlet? Camisole? Her dark, krinkly hair is gathered in a ponytail. It was she, standing at the end of the bar, who had received Romesh Kumar's "please-tell-Mr.-Chutneywala-I'm-late" phone call. She accidentally hit the speakerphone and public address system at the same time, alerting indoor and outdoor customers to a Chutneywala in their presence, and that she thought "Chutneywala" sufficiently amusing to ask for a repeat. Everyone had heard her giggle. They overheard her half of the conversation. *"His name is what? Chutneywala? Come on, man. Who shall I say is calling?"* Everyone also heard "Romesh Kumar." He had no secrets.

He'd pretended indifference when she approached his table. Her head – lips, tongue, ears, nose and eyebrows – was a mass of cosmetic shrapnel. Rings on every finger, thumbs included.

"Mr. Chutneywala? You're Parsi, right?" she'd said. "See, I'm not ignorant. Your friend Mr. Kumar said he'd be a little late."

"So I heard."

"I think he said 'a trifle late,' to be more exact."

To deflect the conversation away from himself, which he knew to be the preferred opening gambit of casual conversation between the sexes in America, he could have asked the meaning of the rows of silver, like key rings of varying sizes, that she wore through her ears, nose and eyebrows – or the large blue star tattoo near the strap of her camisole – but he chose the least obvious: the rectangular, flesh-colored bandage on her shoulder. It reminded him of inoculation shots, international travel and of his own life when it was just opening up and full of promise.

"I see you are going away," he'd said.

"What? The tat? That's from my commune days."

"No, below it, the plaster. You must have had some shots."

"This? It's my nicotine patch. But you're sweet for asking."

"I'm sorry," he said. "It is none of my business."

"No, no, it got so bad I used to smoke in the shower. I had to say to myself, enough is enough already. Hey, I've been to Bombay. I've seen the Towers of Silence. I think it's the coolest thing, putting dead bodies out for the buzzards. You guys don't smoke, right? You're fire-worshippers, aren't you? Maybe I was a Parsi in my former life."

"Fire is a manifestation. Christians do not worship two pieces of wood. We worship god, not fire." It is an explanation he has gone through many times, patiently.

"That's more or less what I meant," she says. "Anyway, I'm not Christian."

With time on his hands, the normally gloomy Chutt can spiral into a full depression. He is thirty-four and unmarried. Giant pandas, Chilean sea bass and Parsi gentlemen suffer a common fate: a deficiency of available females. Insufficient molecular interaction. So few Parsis – just fifty thousand in the world, if that, and dropping – and so much territory to cover. In his own family, among cousins of his generation, not a single boy had found a suitable Parsi girl, or vice versa. His older sister Shireen had gone to Düsseldorf for engineering and married a German boy ten years her junior. After two sons, he'd deserted her for a Turkish girl. Her sons hated India. They hated being taken for Turks on German streets. They'd become skinheads with dark complexions. His younger sister, Freny, was an unmarried schoolteacher in Parsi Gardens, nearing thirty, too old to marry unless she found a foreigner or Parsi widower.

On her next trip past his table, the waitress drops off a plate of Buffalo chicken wings, also on the house. "My name's Bekka," she says.

"I'm called Chutt."

"I know, " she said. "*Please tell Chutt'* ... that's how that Kumar guy who's a trifle late started his message. Frankly, I didn't like him. Here you are, sitting here so patiently. You look so calm. You look like you're thinking profound thoughts. Bekka's short for Rebecca."

"That's a very pretty name."

"Very Old Testament, you mean."

"Good names come from good books."

"It's Jewish."

He lets out a long, low "ahhh." He remembered his best years, standards eight through twelve, at the Sassoon Trust School. When he was eleven, his father sent him down to Bombay from Baroda to live for six years with his Aunt Dolly and Uncle Jamshed Contractor. Jimmy Contractor was called Uncle Two-in-Bush for his failure to keep One-in-Hand. Sassoon Trust had been a Jewish School during British times, but after Independence most of the established Bombay Jewish families started leaving for Israel and England. The Trust is still Jewish, at least in name, but the numbers of Jewish names on the scrolls of class toppers had been yielding to other aspiring minorities: Armenians, Anglo-Indians, Parsis and Muslims. He felt close to the Jews. His old teacher, David Solomon, said the Parsis are the real Jews of India: a dwindling minority, huge in commerce and the professions. With so many Parsi trusts and hospitals, there are no poor Parsis.

It's a curious fate, to be a threatened minority with no visible enemies. Truth be told, Parsis are a beloved minority. Admired, trusted, generous, intelligent and patriotic. Every Indian honours Field Marshal Sam Manekshaw, the Ariel Sharon of India in the '71

War. He remembers Prudence Solomon, called Esther by her father, his first crush. She married Danny Saul from his class, his competitor for topper, and went off to England. Chutt was left alone with the uncontested class medal and his name inscribed for all to see.

"The school I went to in Bombay had those little things on the doorframes ... "

"Mezuzot?" she cries. "Holy shit! Mezuzot in India!"

"We called them Methuselahs. Someone said they were old men wrapped up tight in a sheet. They're scrolls, isn't it? What did we know?" His current house in Squirrel Hill has mezzuzahs outside every door, and he's been afraid, and too nostalgic, to remove them.

Chutt is a Wharton graduate. Mellon Bank recruited him, brought him to Pittsburgh and made him an acquisitions manager. He knows the business very well; his division has posted double digit gains every year of his management. Hundreds of millions of dollars pass through his fingers, figuratively speaking, every day, including that very afterooon. *Our Wunderkind*, the client-brochures call him; he's been a Pittsburgh Top Forty Young executive three years' running. Who couldn't be? he asks himself. For picking winners, he didn't need Wharton, the caseloads, or the anxieties of preparation and presentation. "You've got a Parsi nose," Romesh had joked, meaning (for once) a nose for profit, not the beak-like protuberance that stereotypically clings to the Parsi profile.

For his first two years, he suffered from the disparity between Philadelphia and Pittsburgh, which he explained to his parents as being at two ends of the same state, like, say, Rajkot and Surat. Imagine me out here in western Pennsylvania, so far from clean and civilized Surat, stuck in the marshes of the Rann of Kutch. He used to fly to Philly every weekend, just to walk familiar streets and drop in on old friends like Romesh, all of whom had managed to find positions along the New York-Washington corridor.

Pittsburgh might as well have been Kansas City. Some of his friends, the foreign or more insulated east-coasters, assumed it was in a different time zone. They'd get together for dinners down at Susanna Foo's, just like old times. Now Romesh is making his first trip to Pittsburgh, sent out by the commodities house he works for in Philadelphia. Now it's Chutt's turn to show Romesh the sights of Pittsburgh, such as they are, if he ever shows. Pittsburgh has an advanced transportation network and a funicular from the river-bank up the sheer cliff of Mt. Washington. The top is said to offer a spectacular panorama. There are fine museums and a good symphony, but Romesh is more a hedonist and man of action than Chutt.

Rebecca is at the far end of the bar, talking on the phone. He can't face another chicken wing, but he feels he should wait it out. In case Romesh has an accident, this is the only place in Pittsburgh he can call.

There is something else panda-like about Chutt, comically sad, not roly-poly, with dark rings under his button-black eyes, and ears prone to black tufting. While generally thin, he has the beginning of a small potbelly. His teeth are firm and white, never drilled, only polished. Even when happy, as he normally is, he appears to be pondering grave matters, or to be in mourning. People feel attracted to him and feel safe around him. They trust him with their money and listen to his advice. To Indian eyes he is obviously Parsi – fairer than most Indians, narrow-faced, long-nosed and bright-eyed. He is quiet and contained, a natural gentleman, as Rebecca has observed. Those seem to be rare qualities in American men, and attractive to a wide variety of women. Over the past nine years in America he has not lacked for companionship, whenever he sought it. He's known betrayal, disappointment and occasional danger, but never heartbreak.

When he first came to the United States, Cyrus Chutneywala

learned to hone an explanation before anyone could laugh at his name. It went something like this: back in ancient times, a distant ancestor had made pickles, hot and sweet. In fact, his many-times-great grandfather had been purveyor of condiments to the British garrison. Indian condiments are called chutney. A person who makes them is thus a Chutneywala. His name signifies that he is part of an ancient community in India called Parsi. In Indian languages, Parsi means Persian. Over a thousand years ago, his Zoroastrian co-religionists, fleeing the invasion by, and forced conversion to Islam, landed on the coast of Gujarat, attracted by auspicious flares of natural gas. They were hospitably welcomed, and allowed to flourish. A hundred and fifty years ago, Britishers determined that every Indian – "Hindoo," "Mohametan" or "Parsee" – should have a name, preferably two, and so Parsis, who had never used names, were saddled with place-names, or professions they had long abandoned. No Chutneywala has dipped chilies and mango or sweet-lime slices in over a century. Chutt's father is a surgeon in Baroda. His mother is a Readymoney from a poorer branch of the celebrated Bombay moneylenders. By the time he finished his disquisition on Parsiness, all but a determined minority were too bored to laugh in his face.

His father is so ashamed of being unable to find suitable matches for his son and daughters that he has threatened to atone by going off to Africa to perform free surgery. His mother wants a fancy flat in Bombay. Over the past five years, Chutt has rejected eight marriage proposals from prominent Bombay Parsi families. They were good girls, educated, professional, virginal, but – how to say – *too* good, too boring for his new sensibility. He is not without guilt over every rejection. He might be prolonging his loneliness, but he is also condemning eight more Parsi families to barrenness. In such a way, because of men like himself, a people die. To find a waitress in Pittsburgh who knows about Parsis seems as miraculous as a Bombay girl who might know about the Pittsburgh Steelers. Or Methuselahs on an Indian's door.

She says, "Look, I get off at nine. I'm just filling in for a friend's shift, normally I don't get off till two. I hate to see you filling up on chicken wings and beer. Your friend isn't coming. He called again and I told him you'd just left. I love Indian food. I know a quiet place on West Liberty."

On the drive over, she removes the row of silver key rings from her brow. He supposes they must untwist like wire coils from a spiral notebook. Every day on his way to work, Chutt drives this same block of West Liberty Avenue, yet he has never noticed the large *Gul Mohar* signboard. How could an Indian restaurant exist in Pittsburgh, blocks from his office, without his knowing? Inside the *Gul Mohar*, she pulls him by hand past empty tables and heads directly to the kitchen. The owners are Gujarati, Joshi by name, vegetarian, he presumes. She calls them by their first names, they by hers, she lifts the pot-lids and swirls the steam in his direction. He is lost for a moment in the intensity of childhood memories, he suddenly recalls names of food and spices he'd nearly forgotten, and can see the family cook as a young man, bald old Rupla with his head full of hair, bending down to offer him two or three rolls of khandvi, over which he drizzles warm phorni and mustard seed and says, "Just for you, Baba."

Rebecca carries plates out to waiting customers. When she returns, she unties her ponytail and leads him to the table nearest the kitchen doors. Was this restaurant here yesterday? Will it be here tomorrow?

The nicotine patch, it too is gone. The camisole strap hides the tattoo. "How do you know these people?" he asks. He means: who are they? Or he really means, Who are you? Even more, he wonders: is this really happening?

"I used to work here. I still help out once a week. At least the customers here aren't always hitting on me."

"I hope you don't think – " Chutt starts.

"I picked *you* up. There's a difference." Mrs. Joshi brings a carafe of wine. Chutt is resigned to vegetarian, but for him they have made a special beef dhansak.

"I called ahead."

Such planning, such conspiring.

"I'm a good Indian cook, Chutt."

He's not much of a drinker, especially after three narrow flutes of beer, but raises his glass in a toast.

"To Romesh Kumar!" she offers. "The very late Romesh Kumar!"

They get into the inevitable. Her story: "My grandfather had a cigar shop – Adam Newman's on Centre Avenue. I loved the smell of cigars and cigarettes. My *zeyde* gave me cigarettes so I started smoking when I was twelve. He's still going strong at ninety-two. For that matter, I started everything when I was twelve. And as for names, we're like Parsis ourselves. I have a made-up name. My grandfather had a big long name back in Latvia, but he spent the whole time on the boat studying English and when he landed in New York he said, 'My name is New Man.' He actually named himself Adam Newman, just like Paul and Alfred E."

Chutt doesn't recognize her references. He wonders suddenly, what do you say to an ape that types everything correctly, five perfect acts, but gets the title wrong? Knig Lear. Or types *t'is* instead of *'tis* in the fourth act? Do you pat him on his balding head and say *good enough*, or say *sorry*, and have him go back and type two hundred pages of gibberish?

A far greater tragedy than Shakespeare ever conceived.

"As for men, let's say I'm a little easy. Actually, I'd call myself a regular Sally Sleep-Around. This is your chance to run away. You work in a bar, you get off at two in the morning ... at least I get to choose. It's hard to lead a Sex in the City life in Pittsburgh but people say if I blonded up I'd look a lot like Sarah Jessica Parker."

"I'm sorry, I don't rec ..."

She waves it off. "I think I'll go ahead. Forever Blonde!"

He's fascinated by the row of tiny perforations just above her eyebrow. Her brow looks vulnerable, detachable like a postage stamp. Does the body have the capacity to restore flesh, to forgive trauma? Can a woman who has been possessed by so many men be loving and faithful? How is it that a woman who has been used by so many remains so fresh, so pure? And the pure girls of Bombay seem so stale and lifeless?

"I have an apartment up on Mt. Washington, two blocks from the incline. I can see Aliquippa out one window and Homestead out the other. Straight down, I've got the Point at my feet."

"I've got a view of Temple Beth Emmanuel," says Chutt.

"No shit – my old shul! We've got a bench inside!"

And then it's his turn. The unmarried sisters and himself, and his father's vow to go to Africa and redeem a continent for his failure. There had been a woman at Wharton, an American of Indian origin who slept with him, praised his projects and professed a great if sentimental love for India, then stole all his research notes and passed them off as her own. She had an American boyfriend who threatened to kill him if he protested.

"Cheating in business school? I thought you guys got points for that."

In retrospect, the proudest act of his life was admitting the sex before an ethics panel, naming the girl and her boyfriend, acknowledging his poor judgment and a certain susceptibility to high-risk behavior. All the Indian students shunned him, except for Romesh Kumar. The girl was expelled; he received a reprimand and was exiled to Pittsburgh. The story of his shame would spread and grow with every retelling, and he would never be hired in India.

"Wharton," she says. "Makes us sort of 'Love Story,' doesn't it?"

Before he can raise his hand in cultural surrender, she seizes it. "Just look at those fingers!" she says. "And that long, long nose! A girl notices things like that!"

"Things like what?"

"Sometimes those stubby-fingered guys surprise you, but you're no surprise, Mr. Chutneywala. I'll bet you could perch three barn owls on your thing."

Is this what she expects? "A sparrow," he says. "Two if very young." To himself he thinks of the pain of supporting a vulture. Then she giggles. "I'm *kidding*! You look so tight and worried. Have your dhansak. Have more wine. Think of Mt. Washington. Let's drink to inclines – sorry, you're such a sweetie! Smile! Laugh!"

In the night she says, "This is the only time I miss a cigarette. God do I miss a cigarette! I took off my patch – you noticed? I did it for you."

He doesn't quite know how to respond. No one has ever treated him to such a gift, or such a sign of respect and devotion. He strokes her hair, notices with some satisfaction the human sweat, like his.

"You know what I get off on? It's when the man collapses inside me, when he deflates, and I'm there to catch him. If he doesn't collapse, I can't catch him."

Chutt knows he collapsed. There is no more of him to deflate, he has told her everything, shown her all there is, all he has ever been, all he can be. He has spoken even of his deepest shame, a blasphemous fear of vultures. He has never confessed it – who would listen, who would care? He suspects that he is the only Parsi in the world with this particular phobia. He would rather have his body buried in Pittsburgh than torn to shreds in Bombay. In most settings, even on a pleasant Pittsburgh evening, he can summon the sweet, high summer, midday stench of rotting flesh.

But not tonight as they stand naked above the city, taking in the promised vision: the sweep of the rivers and the orange running lights of barges heading down the Ohio, the lighted arches of a dozen bridges over the Allegheny and Monongahela, the fluorescence of the Point, lights so close he could reach down and touch them, from a place so quiet he can hear their hum and sizzle. He is certain that none of her men have rocked her in their arms like this, as barge lights disappear behind the headlands.

POTSY AND PANSY

1.

ON CHUTT'S BLOCK in Squirrel Hill – a "mature" neighborhood, the real estate agent had called it – twelve houses with generous yards huddled modestly under ancient oaks ("hence the squirrels," she'd said). Each house had at least five bedrooms ("big families in those days"), remodeled kitchens, dark floors, built-in bookcases with beveled glass doors and mezuzot on the doorjambs. ("Culture and religion," she said, "very big in Squirrel Hill"). Squirrel Hill was, or had been, Pittsburgh's traditional Jewish neighborhood. According to Chutt's counting, ten of his block's twelve houses were now owned by recent South-or-East Asian immigrants, nearly all of them em-ployed in the higher reaches of Western Pennsylvania Hospital. His girlfriend, Becka Newman, was a Squirrel Hill girl. Her late father – before abandoning his family and joining a commune in California – had been a violinist in the Pittsburgh Symphony, under Steinberg. Her immigrant grandfather, Adam Newman the Cigar King – who'd taught her to smoke while sitting on his lap – had endowed a bench in the synagogue-community center across the street. Every Sabbath an aged congregation filled the parking lot and shuffled to the synagogue's open door, carrying religious apparel in small purple pillows. Chutt would settle back in bed, reveling in the Saturday morning prospect of a little more sleep, a late morning visit to the farmer's market, and a bistro lunch.

Becka, by night a waitress and bartender at Warhol Square, had discovered the ultimate niche profession. At the request of her new neighbors, she removed painted-over mezuzot. Asians didn't want to slight any god, and so had hesitated to touch the odd little symbols without making a propitiating gesture, or snatch of a prayer, neither of which they knew. "It's a little strange," Dr. (Mrs.) Swaminathan had said. "Even with all my own gods around, I feel someone's still watching us." And so Becka would say a prayer, apply paint remover to the doorjambs, pry out the old ceramic or metal casings, then sand, fill and repaint or re-stain where the mezzuzah had been nailed. She turned her small fee over to the community centre's smoking-cessation program.

Just as his romantic life seemed to be on track and a third plaque in three years confirmed his status as Pittsburgh's leading "under-35" banker, the weight of the world came crashing down on his frail and hairy shoulders, like the nightmare vultures of his childhood, circling the Towers of Silence in Bombay.

The news appeared one morning on an internal email: *Mr. Milton Beloff has submitted his resignation, effective immediately. He will be missed for his long years of dedicated service.*

Like hell, thought Chutt.

Happily, an outstanding replacement has been found within our ranks. The appointment of H. S. Mehta (current director A&M, Boston), as CEO of the expanded Pittsburgh-based Section Two financial services takes effect immediately.

The white Americans went to the man they called Chuck with simple questions. Medwick of Currency Exchange asked, "Mehta – that's an Indian name, right? Like the music guy?" Yes, said Chutt, like Zubin Mehta. But he didn't add, *Mehtas can be Hindu, Parsi, Sikh or Muslim. It's a slippery name. Zubin Mehta is Parsi, like me,* but Medwick wouldn't know the difference, or care.

"Great," said Medwick. "Those guys are really smart. If anyone can move us along, it's an Indian."

Those guys? What about me? Chutt wondered. Despite a thousand years on the job, I'm still not quite Indian? Not quite anything. What message are they sending, those big-time, Section One directors strung along the east coast from Boston to Charlotte, importing this unknown H. S. Mehta from Mergers and Acquisitions in Boston when they had Cyrus Chutneywala, three-time Pittsburgh Man of the Year already in place? Something they know? Something about me is just a little unsavory?

On the flimsy authority of other managers, he was informed that Indians are conservative but flexible and as fast as cobras on a heating pad. Good family men and corporately loyal. They mind their business and are great at numbers. Under Beloff, bonuses had withered. With this Mehta guy, big bonuses are here again. This Mehta guy ("Meetah? Maytah?"), opined Commercial Mortgages McAfee, must be really good if they're moving him up from a single branch in M&A all the way to CFO of Section Two with its sixty branches between Pittsburgh and Chicago and complete banking services in five states.

Chutt smiled, and held his tongue. He'd known many India-born dolts with the reaction time of cobras on an ice floe. He knew them to be endlessly inquisitive about everyone's business, a nosiness covered up by flowery greetings at birthday times. Who but an Indian would learn his employees' birthdays? Why not ask instead: *What does it mean, getting a new boss from Mergers and Acquisitions? What's his slant? Do we want to work for an M&A bubblehead? I thought they were clearing those clowns out of the banking business. M&As damned near ruined the whole economy, and now we're – what? – slip-sliding back into the mergers business?*

The India-born managers had a different take. From Jerry Gupta in Commercial Loans: I like working with Indians. I just don't like working *for* an Indian. That's why I came to America. "H. S. Mehta?" wondered Tony Madhuvan of Currencies. "What's the big secret? Harish? Harbins? Haris?" Javy Qureishi in Residential Loans said he could be one of ours, a Muslim. But the smart money, from Chutt on down, was on a Sikh. "H. Mehta" could be anything, but the "*S*" signaled a Singh somewhere in the name; hence a Sikh: beard and turban, big and hairy.

Becka, who could be counted on to clear the air of ambiguities charged, "That is so fucking Indian of you, Chutt. You wonder what *community* this Magic Mehta comes from? Like if he's Muslim he's going to fire all the Hindus? As if you even care – Parsis are loved. Parsis are always safe. And tell me this: *why* do you assume Magic Mehta is even a man? Did it say *Mister* Mehta?"

The possibility of a woman had never occurred to him. For all the years he'd been in America, he hadn't made the most funda-mental leap to American thinking. Thank God he had Becka to uproot his assumptions. She was a formidable woman. To please him, she had slowly divested herself of the full-metal jacket, remov-ing the facial shrapnel, the nose, lip, tongue and unmentionable rings, the eyebrow clips and half-dozen ear-studs. The nicotine patch had done its work. Even now, without her decorative armor, he deferred to her suspicions.

"So, what kind of a she do you think she is, if she's a she?"

"Who cares? Maybe even a Christian or something."

And then he went up to the study to open his private email. There was the near-daily message from his mother in Bombay. He had told her about Becka. He'd reminded her that they'd sent him to a historically Jewish school, the Sassoon Trust in Bombay, remem-ber? And that Jews and Parsis held analogous positions in their respective societies. Few in numbers, huge in consequence. Buying a house in Squirrel Hill with painted-over mezuzot on the door-jambs and inviting a Jewish girl to live with him was practically pre-ordained. He'd sent that note two weeks ago. Now:

Dearest Chuttu: What do I know of this thing you call love? You love too easily and too often. I pay no mind to your living arrangements. In my day, you got married when your father found you the right girl or boy, and that's the way our little community prospered down the centuries. Your father has worn out shoe-leather interviewing parents with suitable daughters from Baroda and Ahmedabad to Bombay and even down to Bangalore. He has studied hundreds of photographs till he says people will think he is dirty-minded. He has rejected every girl that is not up to your so-called standards of beauty and liberation.

I can now report that he has found a match. She comes from an outstanding family. Her father is Darius Batliwala, who endowed Dadaji Bottlewala Gardens in Bombay and is involved in many charities and trusts. Batliwala Ltd. still bottles water and soft drinks, so the family fortune remains intact. Her late mother was Nazreen Cowasjee, from a respectable family in Pune that endowed the Poona Pediatric Hospital. The girl has appeared in several movies and television shows in England and Canada. Her good name, not her screen name, is Pansy Batliwala, but if you look her up on Google, the name is Darya D'Aquino. She also has a Face Book page you should not be missing (follow this link). She was married briefly, under a year, to a Canadian but is divorced with no children.

She is not unblemished but you turn your nose up at such old-fashioned ideas anyway. She is twenty-five and she exceeds your standards. Her father says she is a clean-living girl and for you to ignore the kind of girls she's forced to play. He says the film-makers see her as "dark and exotic" in Canada, but in India she'd be fair and European. She has only one blemish, the aforementioned marriage/divorce. She lives in Toronto, which I have checked with Mrs. Contractor at the travel agency is less than two hours away from Pittsburgh with no stops, but <u>you must take your Green Card or proof of legal residence with you.</u> Driver's licence no longer sufficient. Her father is agreeable to an unchaperoned meeting between you.

"Our little community?" Guilt, guilt, guilt: Ma, why do you do this to me? You mean our little and shrinking community because my sister married a German and got divorced and I've never even involved myself with a Parsi girl and I've turned down every opportunity to marry one because they've been so ... plain, sometimes plain-looking but mostly plain-living, plain-thinking: goody-goody school-teachers, doctors and academics. "High in state bureaucracy with secure income." Life with any of them would be one long self-sacrificing commitment to social progress.

And then, Baba, how could you, my sober, cost-accounting Parsidoctor father, have discovered a woman like this Darya D'Aquino whose link he had already opened and whose pulsating sexuality now stared back at him? Why didn't you suppress her picture? You know my weakness.

Darya, Darya, Darya. The Amu Darya is a river running through the deserts of central Asia, near the Parsi homelands. The Greek name was Oxus. Darya is a Persian word, a subtle signal to those of us in the know. A better name than Oxus, or Pansy.

It's always the case with Chutt: he breaks away, he's into the clear, dashing to the goal like Fast Willie Parker – forty, thirty, twenty, ten, five – and the whistle blows and the play is dead. A ten-yard penalty, upfield. The community and its obligations have reeled him back.

He locked the study door. Pages of Darya D'Aquino glossies, movie-stills, TV-promos and modeling shots. Links to dozens of "Where To Find Me." She was everything his mother had promised, and more, even discounting the possibility of airbrushing.

Magical Mehta was even more than Becka had predicted. Harriet Samuels Mehta was in her early forties, with green eyes and short, blonded hair. On her first day she went to each department manager and discussed his employment history, like a well-prepped schoolteacher on parents' night. To Chutt she said simply, "Mr. Chutney-wala, I'll have a special proposal for you and your partner ... Miss Newman, is it?"

Is nothing private? He'd attended occasional bank social gatherings, always alone. None of his colleagues had met Becka. He liked to think no one could even imagine them together. Maybe he'd entered into a permanent relationship without even realizing it. His parents had talked to him about their own marriage: *it was five years before I realized I loved him,* said Ma. *It was after you were born,* said Baba. That's the Indian ideal: marriage first, then love will usually follow. If not, there's nothing you can do about it.

His parents had been in their early twenties; he was thirty-four. Maybe Becka was It, the end of his quest. Maybe she was his defining moment. But just as he was about to settle in for the long haul, thanks to his parents' meddling, he'd glimpsed an alternate reality.

Every night he slinked into his study and hit the magic keys. "Hello, welcome to my home page." No accent. "My name is Darya D'Aquino. People ask me where I was born ..." she smiles, with dimples ..."let's just say a little while ago, in a galaxy far, far away." Clips from a low-budget movie where she pole-danced and seduced the hero; more from a Canadian police drama where she gathered forensic evidence. With her hair down, she was sultry, or was it fiery? With her hair in a bun, with glasses, above a microscope, she was Doctor Miss Science. And Chutt asked himself, what am I doing? This is madness. This is a temptation I'm not disposed to accept.

"Now I'm shooting a feature called *Planet-X*, in French with a little English. If I tried to explain it, it would sound hopelessly complicated. Let's say it's a little bit science-fictiony, but I leave it to your imagination what exactly Planet X might be."

On Ms. Mehta's second day, she explained to the managers how she'd got her Indian name. Her great-grandfather, Col. Basil Mehta, Indian Army, was an Anglo-Indian who married a Scottish missionary. Their son, her grandfather, married Dolly Samuels, from a Poona Jewish family. She's ninety-one and still tends her garden in Poona. Her father is a retired electronics engineer at the University of Illinois-Urbana. Her late mother was a German-American from Kenosha, Wisconsin.

"For those of you of Indian origin," she said, "I should warn you that in my backpacking days I did a doctorate at the Delhi School of Economics, and I understand Hindi, Punjabi and Marathi. So if I were to define myself it would be a well-traveled, Indo-European, Judeo-Christian American."

On their first confidential meeting, Harriet Mehta told him she had an offer for him. Did he know there were trusts written up by Parsis in the middle of the 19th century that are earning more income today than they did back then? "Those old Parsis had powerful algorithms."

Chutt responded, "At Wharton I figured out an algorithm for assessing the future value of a stock or a commodity." He didn't mention a woman stole it from him. Or that he'd been involved with her. Or that she was, unknown to him, married.

"I know," said Harriet. "I read it. And to be perfectly frank, I know about the troubles you had with ... what was her name, Ms. Pinto? Water under the bridge; frankly, I admire you for it. Look, I knew three months ago I'd be taking over Section Two. I spent those months reading files. I had some friends at Wharton and I asked them, is this guy for real? They said if you'd stayed in academic economics you were Nobel material. The algorithm for valuing stocks, the algorithm for pricing variables – I stayed with them till those sigmas and deltas got too much. So I told myself, we're not looking over a job applicant here – *we've already got this guy!*"

"I felt smothered in the academic world," he said.

"Let me put it to you this way. You're too smart for Section Two."

I know, I know.

"So what if I were to offer you something in EAT?"

His confusion must have shown.

"Estates and Trusts. Section Four, out in San Francisco. It's small now, but it's a work in progress."

We have a Section Four? "What sort of something?" he asked.

"The whole thing," she said. "We're expanding to California. And we see EAT as a special niche."

He tried to look knowledgeable.

"The first generation Indian immigrants in Silicon Valley aren't getting any younger. They've made tons of money and they've invested it conservatively but they want to retire comfortably to India. They want servants and flat screens and gourmet restaurants and travel and maybe a country house and philanthropies. And they want to leave trust funds for their grandchildren. We think EAT is something we haven't exploited."

"I'm not a lawyer, Ms. Mehta. I've never done estates or trusts."

"You can hire a lawyer. You can hire a dozen lawyers."

"How many EATs do we manage in Pittsburgh?"

"Hardly any. Pittsburgh was the Silicon Valley of the 19th century – can you imagine running Carnegie and Westinghouse and Frick for starters? No, you'll have to relocate out to the Bay," she said. "It's beautiful out there, believe me. We want someone of Indian origin, but it can't look like some weird kind of affirmative action.

That's why I like you for the post. Your resume can stand up to anybody's. And as the head of a major division with untapped potential, I can recommend a doubling of your salary, before bonus."

Darya had written him, in answer to his inquiry:

What a pleasant surprise, Mr. Chutneywala. For better or worse, those pictures on my FaceBook page are new, and un-retouched. I know my father is probably as anxious as yours to get me 'settled.' I fear my father and I have radically opposed definitions of that word – perhaps you share that fear.

I am a traditional Indian girl, despite appearances. Since my divorce I have not been in any long-term relationship, although I must admit over the past three years I have been auditioning a number of possible suitors. I have not found what they call "a suitable boy." I do not despair of finding the right man eventually – only maintaining a reasonably high standard of self-respect as I go through the search.

I will be in Toronto towards the end of the month shooting the English-language segments of the film. I am living in a small apartment on the lakeshore near Harbourfront (any taxi-driver will know the building). Looking forward to our little get-together, if you don't mind sharing our time with a few dozen friends. Darya.

He'd never lied before, but to Becka he'd said, "Something really boring just came up, in Canada of all places. I'll be back on Monday." She didn't ask for a phone number or the name of a hotel. Everything about Becka was compatible, and nothing except ancestry about Darya. He and Becka never went to movies, never even rented them. On television, they only watched the Steelers and Penguins.

He knew nothing of Darya D'Aquino's world. The big names of her life were unfamiliar to him. She'd written him that "Sutherland" was in her new movie, "Planet-X", playing an aged 60's prophet, "a Carl Sagan figure," but he'd never heard of Sutherland or Sagan. "Shatner" – whoever he was – makes a cameo as an outer space skeptic. Witty, no? She'd asked, and he guessed it must be. "Sound of Music" Chris Plummer plays her boss, an "Ottawa Mandarin", whatever that was. Where had he been, these past ten years? No one he knew at Wharton or the bank had ever uttered those names, at least not to him. Nothing he'd ever read spoke of them. Was it too late to catch up? With her, he'd only be able to nod, or make a fool of himself.

And yet, in front of her pictures and reading her letters, he was powerless. What man could resist a force like Darya D'Aquino? And why hadn't she burst his little bubble and written (as he feared, with each new posting), *I'm sure you're a nice man, but you're very scrawny and funny-looking.*

2.

Chutt's thoughts on the flight to Canada: She's Parsi. Beautiful, witty, talented, liberated, and Parsi. Just when I'd given up, they exist. I knew they had to be out there. She's the reason I've been waiting. I can't be blamed.

Toronto, this late March afternoon, was cold but sunny. Spring had already started in Pittsburgh, but salt-pitted old ice crunched underfoot as he exited the terminal and moved down the taxi rank. The drivers appeared Sikh, Caribbean, Chinese, Somali, and Bangladeshi – a variety he'd never experienced in Pittsburgh. Many of the passengers waiting in line were Indian or Chinese, with circulating clots of well-dressed Europeans. From what he'd seen inside the airport, including the customs official who'd stamped his passport and welcomed him to Canada, Toronto was a very large city devoid of white people. The only Canadians he'd heard of were Sidney Crosby, captain of the Penguins, and Mario Lemieux, the team president.

On the long ride from the airport, they passed through a Chinatown, then a second one, and through other ethnic neighborhoods without English signs. He could be any place in the world. He hadn't spoken a word of his native Gujarati or his high school Marathi and Hindi in at least ten years, but something compelled him, in the neutral air of Toronto, to try some Hindi with his pink-turbaned, bristly-bearded, broad-shouldered Sikh driver. Chutt asked, "I've seen a lot of Chinese and Indians here. Any white people?" The driver squinted into the mirror. "Where did you learn an Indian language?" he asked, in Punjabi-accented Hindi. Then he bored deeply into the mirror. "Parsi fella?" he asked, and Chutt pointed to his good Parsi profile and the driver whooped a loud belly laugh. He circled one hand over his head, "Watch out for the buzzards, Brother," he giggled, still circling his hand added, "in this place, not everybody looks Indian comes from India. Lots from Trinidad. Look like India, live like Africa. White people live way outside," and he named places, probably suburbs. As the meter clicked past forty-five dollars, the lake, gray with islands in the distance, opened up between the apartment towers.

In the lobby, a Miss Marcia Wu at the concierge desk closed a thick textbook and asked him his business. "I'm here to see Miss D'Aquino," he said.

"No one by that name here," said Miss Wu. Thank god. He had the wrong address, and he had no way to find her! Fate had taken the meeting out of his hands. She wouldn't be in the phone book. He didn't have his computer. He could turn around and go home and apologize tomorrow.

"Is there another name?" she asked. It was a book on international trade.

"Maybe ... Batli ..."

"Five-oh-two," she said, with a smile, then riffled through a thick reservation book. "Your name is ... Mr. Chutneywala?"

Outside the door of 502 he heard loud voices, male and female, tears and lamentations in a foreign language. Then in English, she: "You lie!" He: "You bitch," then a slap.

And so, he waited. The voices died down to indistinguishable mumbles. A woman's giggle, a man's broad laughter.

After five minutes he rapped softly on the door. It opened widely, almost immediately, without embarrassment. "Mister Bankerman! Right on schedule!" The unmistakable, just-as-advertised but even-more-so Darya D'Aquino. "Welcome to my humble guest apartment." She took him in, up and down, all the details, like an advanced scanning machine, before smiling and shaking his hand.

It was a small apartment, sparsely furnished, on a high floor looking over the lake and a scattering of islands. She was as beautiful as her pictures, if slightly shorter than he'd imagined.

"Very nice place," he said.

"You think? It isn't mine. The studio rents it and furnishes it and I don't even buy the groceries. You want a drink?"

He put up his hand. She stared at his fingers. "You do drink, don't you?"

"A bit," he said.

"You don't mind if I do?"

"Wine?"

A man stood at a bank of windows, back to the door, looking out on the unbroken vista of the lake.

"Al, please be sociable," she scolded. "It's Mister Chutneywala, all the way from ... what was it?"

"Pittsburgh." It sounded absurd, pitiful.

"Red or white?" she asked.

The man turned; the handsomest, the most beautiful man Chutt had ever seen. Indian, but a good size, and maybe Chutt's age. If this is my rival, he thought, the bitch, the slap, there's no contest. The resident suitor seemed to shift through a series of personas before settling on something suitable. Then, hand extended, he approached. "Mr. Chutneywala, I hope we didn't upset you." They shook hands. "Al Neeling," he said. "Or Alok Nilingappa, as you prefer."

"We were rehearsing tomorrow's lines," said Darya. "Big scene."

But tomorrow's Sunday; they shoot on Sunday? Sunday was going to be our day together. He had return tickets for Sunday night.

"It's time to take my leave," said Al. He seemed to wink, or was his face just naturally expressive? "Till tomorrow," and the two actors kissed, most convincingly.

She ran her fingers through her hair. She pulled her tunic straight. He draped his overcoat over the back of the sofa then went to the window, looking out on the lake. This is a mistake, what am I doing here?

"This must be strange for you," she called. "Come here."

And so, of course, he did. She barely came up to his chin. "We have choices. Down here there are some upscale fast food places. There are some great restaurants up in the city proper, any kind of food you could possibly want. Or, we can stay in. The crew fills my fridge every morning, so there's probably something to heat up."

"Staying in is fine with me."

"That's good. Now we have to get over the awkwardness of first meetings. How do you propose we should do that?"

"I have no idea."

"You could start by telling me about your girlfriend. I assume you've got a girlfriend. Let's see, she's obviously an American and probably not a banker. You met her in some public place. If we met, I'm sure we'd get along. She's a little adventurous, right? Maybe even assertive. You like assertive women, don't you?"

"I do," he said. Prior to Becka, Chutt had had three girlfriends, one of them a gold-digging fraud. Becka, as a barmaid, had hit on him. She confessed that she was tired, looking for a good man and security. For years she'd gone through an average of three men a week, at least.

"Those delicate flowers, they're not for you, are they? But, if I may ask, why have you come all this way from Pittsburgh? Why are you pursuing this little drama, or whatever it is?"

Isn't it obvious? Why do you make me so uncomfortable?

But she was smiling. "Why not just come out with whatever it is you're actually thinking?"

"I'm thinking too many things," he said. "You're right, there is a girlfriend. She's much as you described her. She's not a delicate flower."

And I wish I were with her tonight.

"Of course." She waved her hand, as though a crowd of paparazzi were standing by the sofa, "Hey, over here," she pointed to herself, "boyfriends!"

"Like Mr. Neeling?"

"Alok? No, Al's just a friend. He hasn't told me much, but I think he walks ... on the other side of the street. We have a big nude scene tomorrow, or at least I do, with him. It's easier with a guy who's only halfway interested. They're shooting it on Sunday to keep the set half-empty. That doesn't bother you, does it?"

She had a way of challenging him with every sentence: confess! Confess to your passions, your jealousy, your two-timing. Maybe that's how actors lived, everything in the open, the opposite of banking and business. "I saw your picture on the Internet, and you answered my letters and there was a tone to them, a personality behind them that made me laugh, and I couldn't get you out of my mind. That's why I'm here."

"That's very sweet. I'm moved, honestly. Now, here's my solution to the nagging question of initial awkwardness. You start by putting your hands here, just above my ears. And you bring them down the back of my head, to my neck. Exactly. Then down to my shoulders, and then down the front to the top button, here. And then the second button. And you bend down, yes, you're getting it, and I stretch upward to meet you. And there's a bedroom just behind that door. And you're not really that hungry, are you?"

Around ten o'clock they raided the refrigerator. He wore his underpants; she put on a bathrobe, but didn't tie it. He still wasn't hungry, but she found frozen lasagna for two in a takeout aluminum tray with a cardboard top. As he might have guessed, she was endearingly incompetent in the kitchen. They drank wine at the breakfast table while Chutt stared and the lasagna baked. They ate directly off the aluminum. Then came the truncated life-stories: her parents had sent her to Switzerland for high school. She'd learned French, and started acting in French, she married her Canadian and moved to Vancouver and started acting in both English- and French-language television, ironing out her various accents. And then learning a new one, Québec-French, for *Planet-X*.

Yes, she'd had affairs with many actors – names that should have raised his eyebrows – mostly for "group cohesion" she called it, but when necessary, for employment. "You know what they say: an actor's face and her body are public property." Bombay seemed a very long time ago, and very far away. She hadn't visited home in nearly six years. "Well," she said, "Pansy Batliwala's come a long, long way."

And what about Cyrus Chutneywala? He mentioned Squirrel Hill, his secondary school years in Bombay at Sassoon Trust, his Master's degree from an IIT and his Wharton MBA, his disgrace with Linda Pinto, the banishment to Pittsburgh and four years in the wilderness, then the arrival of Harriet Mehta and a job offer to California. What a pathetic resume. Cyrus Chutneywala was going around in circles.

"If it's L.A. we might be in business," she said. "Al loves it."

"I'm afraid it's nearer to Silicon Valley. San Francisco, maybe."

"Vancouver South, we used to call it."

And then there was the silence of an unfamiliar apartment in a new city, after sex with a stranger. There had been a rush to open up and tell everything, and then nothing was left. They had no small talk, nothing shared. He had the feeling that the next person to speak, and the next thing to be said would be, somehow, unanswerable.

"Are you ready for our little talk, Mr. Chutneywala?" And her face was suddenly older, not flirtatious. "Let me say, first of all, you're very appealing, does your Becka tell you that enough? You're so skinny – I like that! You've probably never spent thirty seconds pumping iron, have you? And nature didn't cheat you. I think all the boys I've been with must be on steroids or something. They look like the David statue. A little too much like David. Hands too big, business too small."

David who? he wanted to ask. What kind of business? All of his life he'd known skinny men, men like his father and uncles, skinny men but with round little bowling balls for tummies. It's an Indian male thing. He hadn't developed a potbelly yet, but he would. Maybe he'd jog, or take up tennis.

"But what I want to know is, where do you see yourself in five years? Running a bigger bank and making scads of money and still chasing pretty girls? Or retired from banking and running a B&B? Or maybe you'll be back in India in a huge Bombay high-rise and married to a nice Parsi girl? Or what about Pittsburgh, married to your Becka? I'm not saying we can't have a good time, it's just that a lot of shadows are hanging over you. You feel guilty about being here with me. You feel guilty about Parsis – you think you should save the whole race, don't you? Maybe you saw me as a way of answering the Parsi call and still having a good time. You're ashamed of Pittsburgh, but you're afraid of California. We can't be a couple, with all those shadows. What do you say?"

He poured himself more wine. His mouth was dry, his lips numb. And still she stood before him with her bathrobe half-open. It is an image he will retain for a lifetime. How could any man answer charges from a beautiful woman standing nearly naked two feet away?

"You haven't said where you see yourself in five years."

"I know one thing. In five years I won't be a cutie anymore. I might be a star, or I could be hosting a Vancouver talk show. If it's going to happen for me, it's going to happen in the next two years. And I'll do what I have to do."

With that, she seemed to wink and begin to move from the kitchen, across the living room. What could he do but follow?

3.

Darya and he were sitting in the atrium, waiting for the director. She was unrecognizable behind giant sunglasses, except as an unspecific celebrity who should be recognized. Across the atrium, Miss Wu was still at her station, eighteen straight hours after Chutt had first entered, if she hadn't taken an overnight break.

"I want you to know," she said, "if your father makes a marriage-offer to my father within the next three weeks, I will tell him to accept. We can have the lagan after we wrap the film, either in Bombay or here."

A full Parsi *lagan*, like his parents': he hadn't thought of the staggering complications. He'd attended many Parsi weddings, including his sister's with her German groom; four days of ceremonial bowing and scraping and still it hadn't lasted. Priests, relatives, presents for everyone, religious vows, the proper clothes, inside a temple or in a rented *baug*. Pittsburgh probably didn't have a Fire Temple. Toronto, from his superficial observation, probably did. All of his life he'd been terrified by Parsi rituals, especially anything associated with vultures tearing apart the bodies of recently departed.

"There must be a rental hall in Toronto," he said.

"Plenty," she said.

In other words: Three weeks from now, I, Cyrus Chutneywala, can be married to the most beautiful woman in the world. Could anything be less ambiguous? It left him with a cold feeling up his leg. In further words: I'm sitting in the greeting-area of a strange hotel/apartment complex in Toronto, waiting for the director and co-star of a movie I'm blocked from watching, where my wife-in-waiting will be screwed for public viewing by the handsomest man in the world.

"Why?" he asked.

The wide, dark glasses stared back.

He clarified, "Why a formal Parsi wedding?"

"Maybe because we're Parsis?" she said. "I've already gone through the justice-of-the-peace thing. I've never unpacked my marriage sari. It sits there sadly in my trunk."

"Why three weeks?"

"Because I really should go celibate till the wedding. Three weeks is about my limit."

No long engagement? No chaperoned trips to Bombay to meet the relatives? Then he thought of the horror awaiting him in Pittsburgh: how to tell Becka, how to dodge the plates and cutlery. Chutt to himself: think it over. Isn't she just a little too fine, a little too much, for you? Isn't she candy, gold or flowers, a Mozart, a Picasso, to any man she meets? And aren't you suddenly acting just a little smug and superior? *See what the rest of the world thinks of me! They think I'm worthy of such a woman!* Harriet Singh thinks I'm brilliant, worth a cool half-million before bonuses, or even negotiation. Becka thinks I'm secretly sexy.

Maybe I'm secretly ashamed of Becka. Maybe that's why we don't appear together. An unworthy thought crept up from the depths of his worst self: just wait till the boys at the bank get a load of her!

Followed by a second thought: would I have to move to Toronto or whatever, just to keep other men away? Oh, the torture of it all!

And to all those questions he could answer: *three weeks*. Where's your algorithm for determining true value now?

At eight o'clock the company van arrived, and from it unpacked Al Neeling first, then a smallish, bearded man in a turtleneck sweater and leather jacket, a young woman and a vaguely familiar older man. Miss Wu ran to open the door. Darya stood and started walking towards them, leaving Chutt on the sofa. The group went through the rituals of sweeping hugs and loud air-kisses, even Miss Wu who seemed tangential to the whole operation.

Darya snapped her fingers, and motioned him to join her. "Everybody, this is my friend Cyrus, visiting for the weekend." Then she introduced them, "This is Jean-Luc Carrier, the director, and his assistant, Marie-Louise Tremblay, and of course you already know Al Neeling and no one in the world needs an introduction to Bill Shatner."

He did, of course, but didn't show it. "Bill!" he exclaimed.

"Potsy!" Shatner responded.

Potsy? He let it pass. "You're the one playing the outer-space skeptic, aren't you?" Chutt persisted.

"My life ... my acting life ... is one long monument ... to ... outer space skepticism. No exploration ... no space travel. Above all, no aliens." Perhaps it was his stagy, comic delivery. Everyone laughed.

"I'm afraid I haven't been keeping up with your life, sir," said Chutt.

"No. Apparently, not, Potsy. Where did you say you're from?"

"Pittsburgh."

"Ah."

It was a long, drawn-out "ah," eloquent in its way, maybe a little pitying.

Darya had one last idea. "Cyrus is going back to Pittsburgh today. *Potsy*, really, Bill," she giggled. "Let's get one good picture of all of us together."

Abdul the van-driver was waved inside from his cigarette-break to handle Darya's little silver camera. And so the picture was arranged, back on the sofa: Darya and Al taking the middle, flanked by Bill and Marie-Louise, with Chutt and Miss Wu on the two arms and Jean-Luc Carrier, the director, standing behind them all, hands on the shoulders of his principle actors.

"*Allons*," he said. "Very long, very important day. Very nice meeting you, Mr. Potsy."

And then they were standing alone in the spacious atrium, Cyrus Chutneywala and Marcia Wu. "Do you need to change your reservation? I can call your carrier."

Getting back to Pittsburgh early was a little frightening. Staying an extra hour in Toronto, alone, was positively repulsive. "Let me think about the reservation. What do Canadians mean when they call someone a Potsy?"

She giggled. "It's not a Canadian thing. Potsy's our little name for Darya's boyfriends. Her real name's Pansy, so anyone who goes with her automatically becomes a Potsy. You know, pots and pans."

Just when he'd puffed himself up to a full head of anger and resentment, he was spewing off the walls and ceiling like a popped balloon. I can't even do righteous indignation anymore.

Miss Wu was packing her briefcase. Two books filled it; she had to carry the third. *International Trade. Ontario Medical Legislation. Capital Markets.* "I'm getting a joint Law and MBA." She flexed her arm. "It builds muscle."

In the next few hours, before flying back, Chutt learned to appreciate dim sum on a Sunday morning in a Toronto Chinatown, as selected by Marcia Wu. She'd had a walk-on cameo in the movie, "can't do a science fiction movie these days without a few Asian faces, right?" He learned that the CN Tower, once the "tallest free-standing structure in the world", had been shrinking over the decade because of Guangzhou and Dubai, but from the observation deck one could still make out the vague beginnings of a place called Hamilton. The skyscrapers had food courts featuring at least a dozen cuisines. He saw where some of the white people lived, in miles upon miles of large and small brick houses and apartment houses stretching into the distance. The names of streets and suburbs reminded him of England. He learned from Miss Wu – Marcia, Marcie – that he had an appealing, almost boyish way about him, more like a classmate and not a professor and certainly not an established banker. She liked his naiveté, and his questions made her laugh. She said he made her feel like a slightly older, more sophisticated woman.

ISFAHAN

WHEN I WAS JUST A BOY in Calcutta, my father knew a famous industrialist. They were all members of the Bengal Club, and many's the evening I would spend at my father's table while he and his closest friends circulated, gins and Scotches in hand. I'm one of the privileged youngsters who grew up in the Reynolds Room, under Sir Joshua's portrait. One of my father's oldest friends was a Calcutta-Armenian, Berj Melikian. I was only eight or nine and I'd greet him with a bow, *"Berj Melikian, may his tribe increase!"* and he would take the cigar out of his mouth and bow like a vizier out of paintings from the Mughal past, when our Muslim conquerors had swept into India from Persia, bringing their Shirazi- and Isfahani-Armenian bankers and doctors with them. From his bow he would say, *Young Pranab Dasgupta, I take the dust from your feet, sir!* then make a playful grab for my shoes, which I deftly dodged. He was the most exotic man in the world to me, dark as any Indian, but solidly built, a thick-shouldered bull with a small mountain of a nose. "Armenian" defined the distant shore of human possibility. He seemed straight from the pages of my favorite history books.

Berj Melikian had won the central government's most prestigious business award for leading the nation in export percentage. He was something unheard of in India at that time: a 100% exporter. I imagined stacks of dollars pouring into the Indian treasury – which I thought of as an enlarged version of the dented biscuit tins kept by tea-stalls and sari-shops – the country growing rich and poverty eliminated, all because of my friend, Berj Melikian. That night, I swore to myself that I would be the Berj Melikian of my generation. And I am, that and more. When he entered the Reynolds Room everyone cheered and raised their Scotches, *Hip, Hip!! The Rockefeller of India!!*

We learned a poem in our St. Xavier's days. "To an Athlete, Dying Young." Hopkins, is it – or Houseman? *"The day you won the town the race/We chaired you through the market-place/Man and boy turned out to cheer ..."* I cry whenever I think of Berj, the bowing little boy, and that poem.

His pig-iron foundry out in Asansol was the world's largest manufacturer of blank manhole covers. In those years, no concern was given to pollution; the prize had gone to the dirtiest and crudest operation in the country. He'd shown everyone how India makes money in the competitive world: find a place already hopelessly polluted, find workers who will suffer any privation, undercut the going Slovakian or Mexican price, and roll out pig iron by the thousands of tons. And if the the specs are just a little off? So what – it's pig iron! It's just a blank manhole cover!

For many years we thought that the path to national riches lay in sectors called NIMBY. Thirty-five years later we've reduced the size and weight of prosperity from three hundred-pound manhole covers to feather-light CDs. Every young lady in a call center carries a ton and a half of manhole covers in her purse. The ideas that whiz across the broadband at the speed of light have incredible density behind them. *May their tribe increase!*

We have a young lady in our house these days. A friend of my son, a girl he met in India on a photo shoot who followed him home, with his encouragement. Girls do not interest him *per sé*, but this one he found sympathetic. He took her picture in a dusty northern town and then gave her some names and addresses. She ran away from home and a pending marriage, and here she is.

After the fire we moved into rented rooms just off Haight Street so that I could be closer to the therapists. The soles of my feet were left on that smoldering deck, carrying my wife to safety. Now we're on Clarendon on top of the city with a three-bridge view. A view to die for, the agent said. When I can't sleep, I sit here in the living room reading or merely looking down on the city, the lights outlining the Golden Gate and the Bay Bridges, the lumpy grid of city streets and the downtown towers. So heroic of city planners, holding fast to a grid despite all the ups and downs of San Francisco, as though they were in Kansas City and not in the middle of a small-time mountain range. I keep my feet on the ottoman, wincing even as the air circulates over the tips of my toes.

The pain is most intense at night. I try to meditate my way through it. I concentrate on positive moments. The Calcutta Turf and Tennis Club: I remember running on the clay courts, sliding to retrieve, racing to the net, leaving my feet on the serve, and strangely, the nerve ends do not rebel. I remember the hours, the hundreds of hours of practicing my cricket bowling and batting, running like the wind, bounding into the crease, or twisting my body simply to lay my bat on the ball and protect the wicket. I feel no pain. But when I think of our hiking on Mount Diablo or walking the beach at Carmel, I imagine every twig and stone and grain of sand embedding itself in the scar tissue, opening up new cuts, new infections, and I'm back once more, pipped at the post, as we used to say, sucking my teeth in pain.

I remember a night in the summer of 2001, the ten-year celebration bash for our little communications giant. In that decade, we had grown from a Stanford garage start-up to a worldwide colossus.

At the banquet, the board got me to sing a Valley version of "My Way." We did a little soft-shoe. I kicked my legs up in a modified can-can. A thousand people applauded and cheered. My feet, my poor cinder-crusted feet, don't pain at the memory.

Idle thoughts, reading a book on Indian vs. American marketing strategies, on melding the best of both worlds, looking down on the lighted arches of the bridges and the city streets at night, like a picnic blanket lit by fireflies. I grew up under one system, and came to profit from another. I am the premier product of both worlds, but the child is winning out over the man.

I stopped thinking it was possible to please both models at about the time I started withdrawing from the day-to-day operations. My wife, who'd left me ten years earlier, came back. Berj Melikian died at fifty-two, and I couldn't attend the funeral. Then came the fire, of suspicious origins. I remarried my divorced wife. I'm a new father again. America blew up. I don't know where any of this is heading. I want to stop the pain in my feet and the torment in my head.

In short, I'm not reading a management book at all. I'm reading my autobiography, laid out in charts and graphs.

I made my fortune from the transmission of data in a new and faster way, which is no more inventive to me now than building a lighter, cleaner manhole cover. I want to spend the second half of my life on more productive matters. An Asian Common Market, something to dwarf the EU and NAFTA. At my desk, in my rehab, or just standing on the back deck and watching the city unfold at my feet, I think of other projects in other cities. I have never lacked focus, but now it's deserting me. I feel under assault from this country I call home.

Two months ago, I visited our operations in Pakistan, Calcutta, Gurgaon and Bangladesh. My managers pleaded with me to come back and take control, but I resisted. Our managers don't need me. These days in India, if making money is your goal it's difficult not to succeed. Each year we plan for thirty percent growth and each year the final figures come in at eighty or more. Workforce increases by a factor of three. I don't need help in making money. I need direction in how to spend it.

When I was getting started back in that little student apartment in Palo Alto, we took our ideas to a bank, asking for half a million dollars, and we were turned down. That was my Calcutta training poking through. My professor directed me to one of the early venture capitalists, a non-Indian who'd had a hand in Apple and Hewlett-Packard and nearly everything of consequence in Silicon Valley. Why would such a proven picker-of-winners even take time to listen to a twenty-five-year-old immigrant? He heard me out, read my proposals, and wrote a cheque for five million dollars. We returned him twenty million within the year. That is the sort of person I wish to become.

I sit here, sometimes all night, when the house is quiet and the city seems under a spell. My son is right, but he doesn't know why: I *do* suffer from post-9/11 trauma. Scales have fallen from my eyes. He thinks I am blind to Indian corruption, that I should give up thoughts of returning, but corruption is an irrelevant irritant. High tech is inherently incorruptible. "Corrupt" is the dirtiest word in high tech.

Tonight, after dinner, he staged a little exhibition of his Indian photographs. "Gay India" he's going to call it. Some are quite affecting. A picture he took of that girl is, in fact, arresting. She sits at a coffee house table where there are flies perched on the top of her coffee cup, and the sunlight coming through dingy windows seems to settle on what could be tears. It's a black and white photo, but the north India heat of April seeps through, and you can imagine the din and the coffee fumes, and you can't help but ask why is this girl about to cry?

And here she is in our house, denying all sadness. "That picture was taken on a happy day. I thought I'd be getting married."

"She was responding to my lecture on photography. Tears of sheer boredom," says my son.

There is another shot, taken in a Bombay public men's room. Police are hauling men out of the stalls, some in business suits, their faces are being ground into the floor-slop. You can smell it. And he was there, with his camera and no one stopped him. He is so in the minute, or should I say, so in the five hundredth-of-a-second, that I have no point of contact. Fragile marriage, no grandchildren, here or in India – what's the use of staying on? The Dasgupta family of Calcutta will die out. Twenty years before my daughter grows up, and I'll probably be gone. And my wife is showing signs of becoming like her late father, trusting to god or to fate, head-in-the-clouds, seeing eternity-in-a-grain-of-sand. I am surrounded by people who live outside my understanding of time and space.

I pick up a back issue of *India Abroad*. "New Hope for Indian Cricket" runs one headline, and the accompanying picture shows a young man with a Muslim name, Rashid Imran, already known to the Test Match faithful as "Rash the Flash," whose features are clearly African. Globalization comes to Indian cricket, a place where I'd least expected it, and so I read on. The Flash is Indo-African, born in London to an Indian mother and a Ugandan father. And suddenly the magazine begins to tremble in my hands because I know that mother. Some version of The Flash could have been my son.

I was nineteen and on the St. Xavier's tennis team. But I'd learned the game at Calcutta Turf and Tennis, where I played incessantly with anyone of any age. I played singles with nationally ranked players and mixed doubles with any competitive girl. And the one I favored was Smriti Roy: tall, beautiful, witty, bright, and age/class/caste-appropriate for marriage. Smriti was known as "India Tobacco Roy" because of her father's status in the company. We had been mixed doubles partners for two years, rising through the club ranks, when it occurred to me and maybe to her that we were destined for a more permanent relationship.

It was one of those moments, in a modest, old-fashioned Calcutta sense, when a light goes on and you see everything that has been laid out as smooth and familiar is suddenly jagged and exciting. I remember it perfectly. I was at the net, Smriti at the baseline, and she slammed the ball into the net, just past my elbow. We lost a point, but she ran up to retrieve the ball even before I could scoop it, and when she bent over, and when she turned to toss it back to me, I saw for an instant the entirety of her body as though she had disrobed in front of me. She was as naked to me as if we had been in the shower. It was a lascivious moment in a young man's chaste trajectory. It meant that new terms had been introduced into the rather simple-minded equation of work + study + success=fulfillment. And she saw my eyes assessing her in this new way, and she broke into a smile, which she immediately suppressed.

She signaled her intention rather directly. She indicated that she'd already spoken to her father about me; had I spoken to mine? I said I had (meaning that I intended to), and from that moment, the nature of our companionship changed. We still played tennis; we still had after-match shandygaffs in the Club bar, and with friends we managed to go on chaperoned retreats and to spend hours and hours in the intimate darkness of the Film Society. But in the distant suburbs of Calcutta and in rooms provided by friends, we fumbled with keys and tore each other's clothes off with hunger and violence. Even today, the words "Dhakuria Lakes" can suck the air from any room. We had to rearrange furniture when we left.

When I was accepted to the IIT in Kharagpur, she said she would stay on in Calcutta, earning her Master's in French. We'd both be involved in studies for another two years. When I would get back to Calcutta, presumably with a Master's degree and the promise of a satisfactory job, we'd get married. During those two years, I never doubted that our parents would make the satisfactory arrangements and that Dasgupta Construction and India Tobacco would be merged in the biggest wedding of the season.

When I finally got back from those two lonely years, I suppressed the fact that I'd been offered a doctoral scholarship to Stanford. In bourgeois Calcutta, prolonging one's studentship begins to look suspicious. There are codes: marry or study, but don't do both. What do you intend, young man, marry my daughter then whisk her off to America? What will she do there, without cooks and servants? We re-ignited our affair almost immediately, but for some reason her name never came up in family discussions. Many years later, I found out that my mother disapproved of the tobacco connection, and that my father had heard "certain tales" that cast doubts on her chastity. I tried not to blush. She was out of the running. Then Dr. Arun Mitter, he of the tea estates – Calcutta's most prestigious industry – pressed the case of his youngest daughter, Meena. She too was beautiful and brainy, and caste-appropriate, and willing to take on the challenge of a new continent. And so, in a gaudy ceremony lasting three days, I was married in time to take my wife to Stanford but it was not the wife I'd been planning to take.

The last contact I had with Smriti Roy was at Dum Dum Airport when she was heading off to London for a law scholarship. It was arranged suddenly, just a day or two after my wedding announcement. "I put my life on hold for you," she said. "It's time I put myself first." Then she took my hand in her very firm grip and managed a little smile. "It wasn't all a waste, was it? I hope you'll be very happy with your little Meena." I probably said something sappy like, "At least we'll always have Dhakuria Lakes," in homage to those hours of Film Society screenings.

Over the years, I've wondered about the suddenness of that trip. I've wondered about those "tales" my father alluded to. Everything in the old Calcutta had such brutal ramifications. Any act of love, however innocent, could rise up like a cobra. In those years, women of good standing didn't run off alone to the West without rumors following. Sudden foreign travel=pregnancy. We'd certainly been heedless in much of our lovemaking.

From that airport moment on, we've lacked any contact except for the Calcutta gossip-mill. I heard that she'd married an African Muslim. India Tobacco Roy cut all ties. She took the name Firoza Imran. She had two sons, and raised them alone. She was a lawyer and a strongly left-wing member of parliament. "Firoza the Ferocious," she's called. My parents were too refined to comment on the religious and racial intermarriage, but took comfort in her socialism as a confirmation of all their doubts about her in the first place.

Had she conceived? What about her "second son"? It's idle speculation now, but if I were ever to contact her I would have to ask. In the curious ways of the world as I'm trying to understand it, Smriti and I are still playing a kind of choreographed mixed doubles, well into our middle age. By the time I learned of all these things, "my little Meena" had left me for a string of men, all of them inappropriate but none of them Muslim or African, so far as I know. Hers was a rebellion against me, not our culture – a young wife in an alien country, and my single-minded ambition. Our lives have settled down to a defined shape and substance. Or at least mine did, until last month.

In those lost years before Meena came back, I was often in London. Many's the time I looked up "F. Imran" in the Parliamentary Registry. I could have called, but of course, I was afraid. I was ashamed of myself, and guilty. Such a radical self- transformation can only spring from anger, rage even – against me, against her parents, against the upper middle classes, against Hindu Bengali bourgeois culture. Once, I saw her on the telly. Still an attractive face, but much of it was hidden by the headscarf.

There are so many secrets in marriage. Meena knows nothing of the most intimate moments of my life. And I can't begin to imagine what she was doing in the years we were apart. And my son is from a different planet.

When I came back from visiting some of our facilities in south Asia, I was still of a mind to stay in California and enjoy my second first-marriage and the baby, and our new house, and perhaps fund a few interesting projects in India from long-range. The customs agent flipped through my American passport, observed that I sure do a lot of traveling, to which I merely smiled, to which he reiterated, "A lot of South Asian travel," to which I said, "Family, you know," and he responded, "Family in Bangladesh, Pakistan, India, Malaysia and China?" and put a number on my declaration form. I'm scrupulous about keeping receipts and not exceeding the customs exemption.

This was at JFK. All I had to do was claim my bag and roll it to the domestic conveyor belt, none of it easy without a wheelchair, then move on to the domestic departures lounge. Nothing comes easily unless I'm met in SFO by my driver. But I didn't make it to the conveyor belt. I was still waiting for my bag at the carousel when a uniformed officer came up to me, specifically to me, no one else, and said, "Let me see some I.D."

He was holding a sheet of paper, which appeared to be a faxed photo. He kept looking down at it, then up to me. I still had my passport and customs form out, but he didn't bother to open it. "Not some fake passport. Some other I.D.," he demanded. I travel in loose-fitting Indian clothing, without pockets. My wallet was in my briefcase. When I started to bend over to pick it up, holding carefully to my cane as well, the officer said, "Not so fast there. I don't want you to open that briefcase."

Now I was starting to get irritated. "You asked for more I.D., and that's where I keep it."

He looked down at his fax one more time, then at me, and something clicked. His mind was made up. "I said, back off the briefcase. And give me that stick."

"I can't stand without my cane."

Very evenly he said again, "Give me the stick. Handle end first."

"I refuse."

He waved his hand over his head, and shouted, "Back-up!" and two younger guards materialized. They conferred, I heard "apprehended" and "uncooperative" and "resisting."

"You're coming with us, Abu."

I took a deep breath, as I went through a list of options, all of which began or ended with variants of *do you know who I am? Forbes 500! Hell, Forbes 35!* I can call senators, mayors, cabinet members, lawyers and bankers. My captors would not take it well. "As you can see, I'm standing here peacefully waiting for my bag. I'm not going to leave it here. And I have a domestic connection in an hour."

To which the lead-officer put his hand on the top of his holster. "Oh, you got a domestic connection, all right. I think you can forget going anywhere tonight. I said 'come with me.' You don't want to resist an order from Homeland Security."

I turned away from him and back to the carousel for just an

instant, and in that moment, two more officers arrived, big fellows, and when they had me surrounded – by now, I'd gathered a crowd of waiting passengers and I could hear them murmuring, *they got him ... to think he was on my flight, my god!* – the first officer said, "Check out his feet. He's got something under his socks. You, get down on the floor. Slowly remove your sandals. Then we're going to peel back those socks."

"The bloody hell you are," I said, and with one swift chop to the back of my knees, they had me on the floor. The first officer was shouting at the second and third, "Lock his feet, lock his feet!"

Flashbulbs went off. I was flat on my back and the second and third officers had each grabbed one of my legs, and now they held my bandaged feet in their hands. My feet are medicated, wrapped, and kept under pressure bandages. I've had a dozen surgeries. If I'd had the strength I would have kicked hard and sent the officers flying backward. An instinct told me not to answer questions about my feet. Any explanation would turn on a self-incriminating fact: they indeed had been injured in a terrorist bombing. The fact that I was the victim and not the perpetrator was immaterial.

The first officer knelt down and held the faxed photo in my face. "Is this you? Do you deny it?"

So certain was I of mistaken identity, of their bloody-mindedness, that I turned away from it. My briefcase was held in front of a dog that sniffed it, apparently confirming the presence of some alien nitrates, or spices, then lowered into a bomb-disposal Dumpster. He pushed the fax back in my face.

The picture was of me. Taken from a cellphone, I suspect.

"Flight attendants report you were disruptive. Do you dispute that?"

"Of course I do – for God's sake," I was crying now, screaming, "don't touch my socks. Put my feet down." Of course, they pressed harder.

"Secure the feet! Be careful, he's got a weapon in there!"

I screamed, I roared. The pain was searing. They started squeezing my feet, laughing as I screamed.

"We've got a report that you were constantly messing with your feet during the flight. What's going on there?"
"I have to keep loosening and tightening the bandages. I'm in pain, let me go!" And the damned hound from hell was allowed to sniff my feet through the pressure-socks, and he must have sent an alert because I was jerked on my side and handcuffed, there on the floor of the JFK baggage room.

I've never been so happy to see a wheelchair. Over the past two years I'd graduated from chair to canes, and then a single cane, but when they whisked me and my entourage of officers, dog and Dumpster through the crowds and the doors and into an elevator, I simply closed my eyes and tried to dream of far-off places. Calcutta. Isfahan, the comforts of reversion. My arms were cuffed to the wheelchair. Less than twenty-four hours earlier, I'd been having dinner with the Minister of Technology in New Delhi, formulating a master plan to put India in the forefront of world technology. I wanted to call Meena from my cellphone, but it was in the Dumpster. If I had come in through SFO, I would have called the mayor, or my lawyer, but in New York, all I have is a sister-in-law in Queens.

I made up my mind not to say another word. When they peeled off the socks, I hoped the sight would disturb their sleep for years to come. When they rummaged through the briefcase, let them be impressed by the business cards, the various journals, scientific articles with my name on them, magazines with my picture on the cover, the official invitations, the newspaper articles, and the faxes from the State Department. When they booted up the computer, let them read the letters to and from colleagues around the world. When they opened my suitcase, let them take out my Indian suit and shirts, neatly folded, the medications, and the silk jacket I'd had made for Meena, by her old family tailor in Calcutta.

Of course, they had no interest in any of that. They flipped through the books and riffled the various pages of papers and magazines and tossed them aside. They were of a mind to hold my property, especially the computer hard drive, for detailed inspection and then proper disposal, probably by detonation. They were impressed by my feet – the purple scars, the intricate stitching – as anyone should be, but they ascribed the scars, as I feared, to bomb-making activity. "Play with fire, you're going to get burnt, right, Abu? What were you doing in Pakistan – seeing your friend in the mountains?"

"You don't have the slightest idea of who I am."

"You're using the name of Dasgupta." They had their little laugh. "Dasgupta, what the fuck kind of name is that?"

Well, all right, I got through my night in hell. I missed the connecting flight to SFO and I got my bags back along with a wan apology, and a warning, about feet and flying. I should have been the one to thank them; they resolved my dithering with perfect logic and clarity. I was able to call Meena and tell her my flight from India was late, and I was staying near the airport and would be home in the morning. And that's another secret she knows nothing about.

This girl is a very nervy character. One minute she's attacking everything about India, it's all corrupt, all rotten, and everything about America is great and good and even glorious, and the next, she's weepy with nostalgia for just about everything in India that even I find appalling. My son and Meena seem to get pleasure and much amusement from her company, so it's hardly up to me to make a fuss.

I'm sitting with my feet up in the dark living room in the middle of the night when the girl comes up the staircase, holding her empty water glass. "Oh, Dr. Dasgupta, you gave me such a fright! Can I get you something? Water?" She doesn't know I can't sleep, or the pains.

"I'm fine. I'm enjoying the view." It's a clear night; the amber lights of the Golden Gate are twinkling. The city sparkles. She drops to one knee and stares with me. She's in her sleeping clothes, a T-shirt and sweatpants, no robe, no bra. It's an innocent but suggestive scene. I'd hate to explain it if Meena were to come upon us.

"May I ask a question?"

She has an appealing directness, I'll give her that.

"Are you thinking of going back to India?"

"I think most Indians have very strong ties."

As soon as I say it, I think: but my wife doesn't. She has strong memories of India, but when she visits, she's unengaged and mainly irritated. She's able to compartmentalize, or maybe just pinch off what she doesn't need. Deadheading the past, like a good gardener.

"All of my life I dreamed of getting to America. Now that I'm here, I don't know if I want to stay."

I could say, a little cruelly, what makes you think you have the option? Tourist visas run out. Instead, I say, "'All of your life?' All eighteen, nineteen years?"

"I'll be twenty in a few weeks."

I'm beginning to feel a slight discomfort. I reach down for the *India Abroad* to cover myself. She cocks her head as though to read the headlines, then glances up at me, knowingly. She's enjoying my discomfort. She should be downstairs, trying to seduce my son.

Meena was twenty when I married her. Smriti was twenty when she left for England.

"Your son is a very good person. He saved my life, you know."

"He tries to be, by his lights. But I don't know anything about his life-saving skills."

"I'll tell you some other time. Some other night, perhaps." And with that she walks over to the fridge for cold water and gives me a little wave, a fluttering of her fingertips, as she goes back downstairs. I have exceeded the achievement of Berj Melikian a thousand-fold, a million-fold, but I remain the lesser man. I will never fill a room like Berj Melikian, even with a thousand shareholders cheering. Man and boy will not turn out to cheer. It's Houseman, not Hopkins, and I can't stop the tears.

I haven't moved in hours and have barely spoken, but my heart is racing, as though I'd climbed the very steep hill below me.

MAN AND BOY

AMERICA HAS GIVEN ME more than I ever wanted, more than I even thought I could want, and I will be forever grateful.

Thirty years ago I came to Stanford to gain engineering knowledge that I could put to practical use. Of course I was planning a comfortable life for my wife (whomever my father might choose) and children (should I be so blessed). Those things, the monetary things, have worked out beyond all accounting. None of that, on the scale I have enjoyed, would have been possible anywhere but America.

Coming from Kolkata, the old Calcutta – in my case, even from well-off circumstances – I'd been formed by life-and-death dangers that define survival in that city. In California, I appreciated personal security I could take for granted, the friendliness of landlords, neighbours, fellow students and professors, and the respect that was paid to me – even as a foreigner – by the business and investment community. I could go to a bank with good credit and a business plan and compete for a loan. In America, I could trust in contracts and know that they actually worked for mutual protection. I cannot imagine a more hospitable country than the United States of the early 1980s.

America gave me everything I ever wanted. But somehow, I, or America, could not deliver on what I really needed. In the spirit of honesty, I must say: it has become time for me to leave.

On the streets of my childhood, I also knew love and security. Back in those days, Sunny Park was green and serene, the bungalows widely spaced behind high walls. I knew the names of chowkidars who night and day sat on wooden stools in our neighbours' driveways, and the danda-walas who walked the street by night, hour by hour, chiming their thick wooden dandas on the concrete, waking us to the reassurance that no miscreants had breached the security of our streets and walls.

We were trusting souls.

I was the little boy in a St. Xavier's white shirt, gray shorts and a loosened tie who would sit at the feet of gnarly old chowkidars, absorbing the people's history of Bengal. The old men's memories and passions stretched back before Partition, to their youthful love for the leader of the Indian National Army, "Netaji" Subhas Chandra Bose. Netaji saw the mortal threats to Britain from Germany and Japan as the God-given opening for India's immediate independence. Allying himself to Britain's enemies – what could be more obvious? According to Bimal Nag, my toothless, chowkidar-informant, Netaji broke with those Congress Party traitors, Nehru and Gandhi. Nehru was even ("pardon me, young sir") on intimate terms with Lady Mountbatten. What kind of Independence could such a twisted man negotiate?

"We know, don't we? *Bishwasghatak.*" Treachery. "Mountbatten's vengeance on Nehru was slicing us up in Partition. They robbed us of our homeland. Your people are from East, no?" Yes, they were. I was born in Kolkata, but both of my parents were born in Dhaka. At home we spoke the eastern dialect and in soccer we lived and died with East Bengal.

Those had been thrilling days in old Bengal, when the Japanese Army was raking through the jungles of Burma to the edge of

"British" India. Soon, the Japanese Army would link up with Netaji's INA, Calcutta would welcome them, and Delhi would automatically fall to our home grown liberators. The British and all the vermin who'd sided with them would be swept away to England or Australia. My grandmother remembered – with mixed pride and terror – the Japanese bombing of Kidderpore Docks. "They meant no harm to Indians," her father had assured her. "Their fight is only with the Britishers."

We hadn't yet learned what the Japanese had done to their fellow Asians in China, the Philippines, Korea, Singapore and Indonesia. Indian nationalists like my grandfather would have called those pictures of bombings and beheadings "Churchill propaganda". He trusted only his two heroes: Netaji and Adolf Hitler. My father remembered his first meeting with American airmen, running up to them in welcome, and being offered a few paise to shine their dead-cow shoes, an untouchable's job. He was a proud man: he never forgot.

Today, Kolkata's airport, (which used to be called Dum-Dum, after the village where the British made their bullets), is named Netaji Subhas Chandra Bose International Airport.

One morning, as I walked past him on the way to school, Nirmal Nag didn't snap to attention and offer a fake-military salute, as he often did. He was slumped against the wall, head nearly in his lap. I walked over to him, asking, "Mr. Nag, are you keeping good health?"

A necklace of dried blood stretched across his throat from ear to ear. You would think that was enough to alienate me forever from my hometown.

At dinner, my father declared, "It seems our Maoist friends are sending a message." But what "message" were the Naxals sending, murdering a patriotic old man and wiping out the only history book I could trust?

"Naxals!" my mother cried. "They'll kill us in our beds. They'll feel our soft hands and kill us on the spot!" The Naxalites were our local Maoists. They wanted to exterminate all educated, soft-handed capitalists like us.

"It must have been a garrote," my father explained. He spelled the word. Nag's death helped me learn a useful new word, never to forget it. "Fear not," he said. "The police will protect us." My father was very friendly with Mr. Ranjit Gupta, the Chief of Police.

"Army and police are all with the Naxals," my mother persisted.

My father was an avid golfer, a member of two clubs with 18-hole courses; one of them designated "Royal." His threesome was usually made up of "Slicer" Sinha, his personal banker, and Dr. "Peppy" Peppermintwala, his arthritis man. When I was twelve, I was allowed to carry my father's bag, and then to scour the greens and roughs for old golf balls. I was present the day "Slicer" laughingly said, "Now I will demonstrate the rationale behind my nickname," and proceeded to skewer a drive into a dense strip of scrub and trees. Just beyond the trees, on the other side of a high wall topped with barbed wire, we could make out the tin roofs and smoke from the cooking fires of a teeming bustee. That's how it always is in Kolkata: splendor and squalor cheek-by-jowl.

Slicer Sinha went to assess his lie, and never emerged. A few months later, when my father thought I could absorb the news, he casually mentioned that two days after the unfortunate incident, Slicer's head, wrapped in an old sari, had been deposited on the lap of his dozing chowkidar. The poor old man went mad.

And I was friendly with the dhobis carrying a family's laundry on their heads, and the istiri-walas – the ironers – standing under broad trees, dropping hot coals into the belly of their heavy appliances to keep them steaming-hot. I knew the names of their children who would sit at their father's feet with a notebook, keeping accounts. The children, somehow, had learned to read and write (as their fathers never had), and to add, and I don't think those children ever missed charging for the ironing of a sheet, a school uniform, a sari, or was any item ever lost or over-charged. My mother double-checked every expense. That's the old Calcutta: double-check, then verify.

If I'd been able to put two-and-two together, I would have placed those dhobis and istiri-walas and their big-eyed children under the tin roofs of the bustee next to the golf course. I would imagine them drawing tea-water from a rivulet where thousands of people had dumped their night's slop-buckets, where wives and mothers squatted for hours turning chapattis and stirring a pot of daal on an open fire fueled by cow-dung patties plucked by the delicate hands of diligent daughters from the dust of roadways. I can still smell the acrid smoke, augmented by millions more street-dwellers cooking the same items by the same cow-dung on the streets of Kolkata, which would turn our winter skies black with smog.

But I was a St. Xavier's boy, skipping along the wide footpaths under a canopy of trees, without a care. It came to me much later, when I'd made my fortune, that I began thinking of the millions of such children in India: bright, curious, adaptive, and how we'd wasted their lives. Back in the days when I could walk without canes or assistance, I toured those bustees. I might not be able to alter the country's fate, but a few million dollars entrusted to an honest contractor could provide clean water, trees and gardens and school rooms with computers and dedicated teachers.

My wife called it a pipedream.

Even today, especially today and the past few months, I can conjure the smell of coal-fired ironed sheets, my mother's saris, and my school uniform. I knew our driver, Naseer Ahmad, and the names of his twelve children and three wives, and our Christian primary cook, Samuel, whose wife and children lived somewhere in Orissa, and Mohammed, our replacement cook, or sous-chef, as I learned to call him, who took over during Samuel's month-long Christmas and Easter breaks.

The major Christian holidays made serious demands on Samuel's time. At Christmas, and at Easter, many of Samuel's children magically found their way hundreds of miles to Kolkata, to Sunny Park, and materialized on our verandah with their hands out. So did Naseer Ahmad's and Mohammed's at Id. With a domestic staff of Hindus, Christians and Muslims, we were always short a driver, a cook, a bearer or chowkidar. We were not a particularly religious family, but we were communally tolerant. We were Hindu and we knew our *gotra* and tried not to violate it by ill-considered marriage. My family had expended all their energies getting out of East Bengal, settling in Kolkata and educating their children.

My father earned his electrical engineering degree in Britain, in the uncertain years just after Independence. India dithered. Should we align ourselves to the East, West, or stay neutral? Socialist, Communist, Capitalist? We were a little of each. And so, four dreary, hopeless decades passed, with Five-Year plans, promises and no delivery. The energy of two generations was wasted, their aspirations thwarted. We fashioned a culture of bribery. We created the land of eternal legal stalemate. We became a stagnant pool of incredible talent, turning cynical and corrupt.

Before leaving for London, my father had married. When he returned he went to work at Calcutta Electric Supply Company. He created a family: my oldest sister, born nine months after marriage, then two more girls after his return, then two boys, and me, the baby. By then – we're up to the early 60s – he was able to leave CESC and start his own company, Dasgupta Electric, which he merged with his father's Dasgupta Construction. We built housing then furnished them with television sets and the transistor radios and recorders and later, microwave ovens. Eventually we eliminated the need for istri-walas, dhobis and door-to-door appliance repairers. Dasgupta C&E was the company that I was sent to IIT-Kharagpur, then to Stanford, to bring into the late-20th century. In my father's incessant planning, my job would be to transform DE&C from retailers into manufacturers and salesmen into researchers.

How orderly and planned my life was to become! If I picked up all the bread crumbs scattered by my father – if I'd come back with the proper engineering degree, topped perhaps with an MBA, if I'd taken charge of Dasgupta Construction & Electric and hired my brothers and brothers-in-law to impressive-sounding positions, if I hadn't fallen in love on my own – I would have led a comfortable and doubtless, rewarding life. I would have been one of Kolkata's young shakers and movers.

I'd already discovered Smriti Roy, the girl I wanted to marry, but it never happened. I went to Stanford instead and she went to London and became a Muslim parliamentarian. Eventually, I married my father's choice, Meena Mitter, and we have our son, and she divorced me and we got back together, for a while, and we now have a baby girl. And we have a second divorce.

Without a drop of rebelliousness in me, I systematically rejected every nugget of fatherly advice. I left Stanford before my degree. I didn't go to business school. I went deep into debt to start my own company. Our son is a very different kind of genius. One night when he was sixteen, in the midst of the usual Indian immigrant "Harvard-Cal Tech or Stanford" debate, he announced: "I'm gay. The whole world will be my university." He dropped out of high school and went on a bus-and-walking photographic safari of India. He took pictures – high quality, I must admit, and much honoured – of all the places boys from good families had been taught to avoid. All the kinds of men and boys we'd whispered about. I hated myself for thinking: thank God my parents are dead. They will never see those photos of men dressing as women and men-on-boys and police raids on rail-station toilet stalls.

My father used to say, "When Manik is turning a picture, all of Calcutta is working." This was never truer than the years of my adolescence when Manik-da – or, as he was known outside Bengal, Satyajit Ray – was making movies based on the novels of other friends of my father, Sunil Gangopadhyay and Moni Shankar Mukherjee. "Shankar" was Bengal's most popular novelist, but with him novels were only a hobby. By day, he was an executive with Dunlop's. Manik-da's films of the 70's were contemporary, not historic, appealing to a middle-class audience and based on the daily compromises made by middle-class, commerce-based Calcuttans. In other words, movies were being made about people like us, like our clubs, our colleges and our class.

When Manik-da was making a movie, all the taxi drivers, caterers, carpenters and electricians, all the part-time and full-time actors, the musicians who'd put away their instruments or packed away their dreams, found work one more time. So did the street-cleaners, repairmen and technicians. Dasgupta Electric provided the appliances and the generators. Middle-class Bengali-speaking children found walk-on parts. Has any artist ever been so attached to his city? Maybe Samuel Johnson, as I learned at St. Xavier's, but I doubt even Doctor Johnson knew such connection, or received such adulation. "When you are tired of Calcutta, you are tired of life," he might have said, had he known our city. Even I found a small walk-on, in *Simabhaddo*. For a few months, I thought of myself as an actor-in-training, dazzled by Sharmila Tagore, not an apprentice electrical engineer. I have known many of the world's "great men" but in my mind, Satyajit Ray was the greatest.

Now I want to be Manik-da. Not to make pictures, but to count in the same way to my city, to be once again connected. All my life I've been a hero-worshipper. I know I can't put this in print, but what I want is to be beloved in Kolkata, like Ray, like Netaji, like others I have known. But I left Kolkata, and all I have is money, and money never makes you happy, or loved.

My editor says, be ruthlessly honest. Be so honest that you might have to change the names and locations and maybe even call it a novel and not an autobiography.

Kolkata, with all its dangers, brings peace to my soul. America, with all its protections, is the more dangerous place. It has deranged me. It has taken away my son and my wife. It has left me in a wheelchair, pushed by a girl of twenty. Security and danger are reversed for me. A gated community in California is the most dangerous place in the world.

After Meena divorced me, she lived with many men. In those years, I also made many missteps. I called it "growing." When I was a so-called "free man", and one of the Bay Area's "most desirable bachelors", I tried to live up to the billing. This time, Meena refused to go back to India with me. She's the true American. She was able to shed her old Indian identity, which I couldn't do. She fell in with American feminism. I could only redeem my error-prone life through the application of lavish charities.

I've been through Heathrow, that ghastly catacomb, hundreds of times. And during the hours I've been left alone, I've sat with the telephone on my lap, thinking of Smriti Roy, the woman I didn't marry, the woman with a "spotless reputation" that I alone besmirched. In England she became Firoza Imran, MP. We haven't spoken in twenty-two years, the day she left from Dum-Dum for a new life in London. For one year in Kolkata, we frolicked like Australopithecines just down from the trees.

She's Muslim, headscarf and all, a junior cabinet minister on the left wing of Labour and a divorced mother of two. One son is half-African, Rashid Imran, "Rash the Flash", a footballer, son of her Ugandan ex-husband. But who's the father of the other?

I've always believed, when I saw her that last time at Dum-Dum and she said, "I guess I'll wake up in Heathrow", that she was pregnant. Now, I'm free. A bright young Parsi banker has locked my fortune into a Foundation. My wife and children are well looked-after. I'm Executive Director of my own Foundation, meaning I can spend my money but no one else's.

This time I made the call. Her secretary put me on hold, then said, "Miss Imran wishes to know your name and business and residence address." I said, "My name is Pronab Dasgupta. She will know."

After a click, Smriti spoke, "So, you finally want to talk." Her accent was perfectly English. Twenty-odd years in England, why wouldn't it be?

"I'm very sorry for not having called," I said.

"Why ever should you? I never thought of calling you."

"I'm going back to India, permanently."

"So, you've left your Meena? Poor thing, thrown out on the footpath without a penny? And I hear you have a much younger lady with you. What are they called these days, trophies?"

"She's my secretary." I'd been in England less than an hour. How could she know?

"Pronab, dear, try not to lie. If not to me, at least not to yourself."

"She's a friend of my son's and she helped around the house. But she got homesick for India. There's nothing between us."

I waited for her response, but the air was dense and challenging. I counted her breaths, as she must have been counting mine. Finally I said, "I'm not lying."

But I was lying. I heard it in my voice. Nothing had occurred between us, but the will was there. She flirted. And I keep thinking about it. A middle-aged man in a wheelchair, a pretty girl pushing him; I could read the faces and smirks of passersby.

"How ghastly for you," she said. "So near, and yet so far. Twenty, is she? Go ahead, there's no guilt, is there?"

"Smriti? May I call you that?" She didn't object. "I'm going back to Kolkata. I've set up a Foundation and I'm going to distribute all the money I made in America to the places where we had factories. Bangladesh, Malaysia, Cambodia, Bihar, Orissa, Bengal. Yes, I'm a guilty immigrant. I'm a very lonely, very rich, very guilty immigrant. And if you ever find yourself tired of Britain or looking for new work, I'll make you the managing director ..."

I couldn't tell if she'd hung up. "Smriti?"

"Excuse me, my jaw keeps dropping. Your arrogance is truly staggering. First, Pronab, there is no Smriti. She's gone, as though she never was. You think you're so persuasive that all you have to do is ask and I'll pack up my life here and go back with you, isn't it? You want me to impersonate Smriti Roy, but she's been dead for twenty years. Don't you see how disturbed you are, how seriously fucked-up, to use your vernacular? I'll be here till the voters throw me out, and then I'll go back to my law practice."

I carry an image, the two of us naked, our borrowed room slightly askew, and I am holding her breasts and she backs into me, and the music begins again and we're at it, helplessly. What I want to ask, I can't. Your other child, the older one, who is he, where is he? Is he ours?

"Firoza ... I'll get used to it."

"That's one small step."

"If I write, you'll respond?"

"I always respond. I'm a politician."

"I mean more than letters. I want to put my life in focus."

"A book? Sounds enchanting. If you're really serious, I'll give you the name of an editor. She even lives in Goa."

I can't say it's a tragedy, especially not a collective tragedy for all the Indian immigrants of my generation, but we had no American childhood, no Archie-and-Veronica high-school romances and no "adolescent" memories at all. We had one long childhood, more or less homogenized since we lived in the same city in the same kind of neighborhoods and went to the same schools, and our childhood ended abruptly with college, and college ended with marriage.

When we arrived in America we were newly minted, without the movies and songs and sports and television shows that form the very essence of American character. We could learn to imitate Americans, but we never understood "It", the essence. Back in St. Xavier's we thought we knew everything. We were taught to be upright men in a fallen universe. We were taught that nothing of importance in the world had escaped our notice. And that is true: nothing of value had escaped us. All that we missed was the trivia, the silliness – in other words, the essentials. I felt like a well-trained spy, convincing in every outward manifestation, but inwardly afraid of exposure.

We were cleared to begin our lives anew in America, free of inhibitions, guilt or family obligations. And (of course) we soared, but we were untethered to any earth. There is a time in one's life when the skipped years come back to claim us. The house I bought had a wine cellar. And with a cellar you're obliged to fill it. And when it's filled, you have to drink it.

I came back to Kolkata, a city so radically changed, so expanded in its suburbs, so redeveloped in its core, so crammed with high-rises, so attractive in new ways with shopping malls, markets, parks, yet still respectful of the staid, quiet ways of my childhood – and, yes, still overcrowded, still filthy – that I had to rent a hotel room for two months just to reacquaint myself. Neighborhoods that had been deeply suspect, areas we would have avoided in my childhood had become the New Kolkata, home to high-rise luxury, garden paths, pools and nine-hole golf courses. Bursting, I might add, with money like mine, earned in the West, the returnees demanding Western amenities, Sub-Zero refrigerators, flat-screen televisions, dishwashers, and of course, blinkers against the myriad varieties of local misery.

I am walking again. On the street (given the perils of broken sidewalks), I still lean on a cane, but inside I walk unaided. My balance is a little shaky, but there's no pain. It's taken a year and many visits from an ancient homeopath, a "nerve doctor", who mixes pastes and applies them to my feet for an hour or two, then washes them off with fragrant oils. I have never been so well attended. My brothers and sisters have risen to a certain metropolitan prominence; they fill in the gossip-gaps and information-underload from my twenty years' absence. They also provide me with reliable drivers, cooks, and maids.

They ask: do I miss America? Their children, my nieces and nephews, are nearly all settled in the States: doctors, lawyers, researchers and economists. Half of Kolkata, half of all India, it seems, are States-settled. My oldest brother, now retired from

Dasgupta Electronics, spends six months with his daughter and her family in Florida, comes home for Durga Pujah, then leaves for another six months to stay with his son and family in Ohio. They make such dual-track adjustments seem so natural, as though boys from the old Sunny Park and St. Xavier's were raised on exotic expectations of travel and cross-continental settlement. In the old days, my oldest sister, widowed just short of her sixtieth birthday, would have worn nothing but white, would eat nothing but rice and yoghurt and live out her life in a poky little flat, maybe with the company of a widowed servant. Now she stays in Kolkata for the "autumn whirl", the social season, then heads off to Italy and France on wine and art tours.

I have made my first targeted contributions. Three schools are nearing completion, one in Bangladesh, one in Orissa, the third in Bihar. Bricks and pipes are easy to procure; finding honest contractors and dedicated principals and teachers and politicians not seeking bribes – bribes on top of bribes, someone bribed on my end to push the project while others are bribed to stop impeding it – that's the hard part. The impossible part, my brothers say.

So yes, there are many American things I miss, like accountability and an honest bureaucracy.

It's beautiful in Goa. The editor that Firoza suggested, Ms. da Cunha, is a taskmaster. She is my age, but heavy and in a shapeless dress, shorthaired, with simple loop earrings. She met me at the airport and drove me to her seaside bungalow. The car smelled of cigarettes, but she did not smoke, at least in my presence.

Another woman, British I'd guess, welcomed us in, and I understood immediately their domestic situation. Out on the verandah, I saw the thick manuscript I'd sent her. We took our seats, her friend served us drinks, and then she began: "The world is not interested in another rags-to-riches autobiography, especially not from the Third World. The next World's Richest Man will be Indian – so what?"

"I will change," I said.

"I want the part of your life before you controlled it. I want the old Calcutta. I want the frustrated energies of old Calcutta, the paths that were blocked, the mindless pieties paid to Netaji and to the British. The luxuries and the Naxals, the reverence to Ray and Tagore, the privileged life led on the margins of danger, the falling into love and lust (but change the names!) those are the foundations of any story. The bad old neighborhoods were far more interesting before they got gentrified. How you built your fortune – leave that to the business pages. How you lost your marriage, let them go. Especially the problem you have with a gay son – cut it! What are the real things that gnaw at you, Pronab? – that's what we never hear from immigrants, that's what we want to know. There are men from India, from China, from all over the world just like you, brilliant men, accomplished men, still nursing grievances, nursing unrequited lust, bitterly going through the motions. They carry scars; they're hollowed out. I know them. I'm one of them. We've bridged huge gaps, but parts are still missing. Few of us, and I include myself, have known peace."

Half of my book, the easy part, had just been cut out.

Over another set of drinks, and another, she said, "I'm a friend of Firoza, as you know. I know all about you. Thanks to you, she said, 'no vow is sacred'. We used to chat in the back taxis on the way to parties and devise tortures for you. 'May his toes grow into a single sharp scimitar.' But I'm also a friend of Smriti. I was a constant companion in London that first year. You might not believe this, but she and I were once the 'It' girls. We were young and cute and available. We were exotics. London wasn't yet Londonstan. We were everywhere and we were seen with everyone."

Every word a knife to my heart.

"Then as you know, it caught up with her."

I nodded, as if I knew.

"He wanted her to abort it, but she refused. So, baby Willie. That was the turning point for her. But he's a joy, isn't he?"

"Willie," I said, nodding sagely.

"That's when we began our little affair. I loved Smriti more deeply than I've loved anyone in my life. It was sudden, and it took us both by surprise. I've stayed on that course, but she couldn't. That's why she married Abdul and changed her life completely."

We discussed this over drinks, under a fan on a cool verandah, overlooking the glassy sea.

ABOUT THE AUTHOR

Clark Blaise (1940–), Canadian and American, is the author of 20 books of fiction and nonfiction. A longtime advocate for the literary arts in North America, Blaise has taught writing and literature at Emory, Skidmore, Columbia, NYU, Sir George Williams, UC-Berkeley, SUNY-Stony Brook, and the David Thompson University Centre. In 1968, he founded the postgraduate Creative Writing Program at Concordia University; he after went on to serve as the Director of the International Writing Program at Iowa (1990–1998), and as President of the Society for the Study of the Short Story (2002-present). Internationally recognized for his contributions to the field, Blaise has received an Arts and Letters Award for Literature from the American Academy (2003), and in 2010 was made an Officer of the Order of Canada. Blaise now divides his time between New York and San Francisco, where he lives with his wife, American novelist Bharati Mukherjee.